Anonymous

Memorial of Samuel Gilman Brown

Born January 4, 1813, died November 4, 1885

Anonymous

Memorial of Samuel Gilman Brown
Born January 4, 1813, died November 4, 1885

ISBN/EAN: 9783337140663

Printed in Europe, USA, Canada, Australia, Japan

Cover: Foto ©Raphael Reischuk / pixelio.de

More available books at **www.hansebooks.com**

MEMORIAL

OF

SAMUEL GILMAN BROWN, D.D., LL.D.

Born January 4, 1813

Died November 4, 1885

NEW YORK
1886

Samuel Gilman Brown.

SAMUEL GILMAN BROWN was born at North Yarmouth, Me., January 4, 1813 ; was graduated at Dartmouth College in 1831 ; was teacher in the High School at Ellington, Conn., from 1832 to 1834, and Principal of Abbot Academy, Andover, Mass., from 1835 to 1838 ; was graduated at the Andover Theological Seminary in 1837 ; travelled in Europe and the East from 1838 to 1840 ; was Professor of Oratory and Belles-Lettres in Dartmouth College from 1840 to 1863, and of Intellectual Philosophy and Political Economy from 1863 to 1867 ; was elected seventh President of Hamilton College, November 6, 1866 ; accepted, and entered, in April, 1867, upon his duties in the Presidency and the connected Walcott Professorship of the Evidences of Christianity ; was inaugurated July 17, 1867 ; laid down these offices in June, 1881 ; was Instructor in Intellectual Philosophy in Hamilton College from January to April, 1882, Instructor in Intellectual and Moral Philosophy and Political Economy in Dartmouth College from April, 1882, to June, 1883, and Provisional Professor of Mental and Moral Philosophy in Bowdoin College from September, 1883, to June, 1885.

In 1827, and before entering college, he had united with the Congregational Church at Hanover, N. H., from whose roll his name was never removed. After preaching for some years as a licentiate, he was ordained to the Congregational ministry at Woodstock, Vt., October 6, 1852 ; he was a member of the White River Association, from which he was received by the Presbytery of Utica, January 28, 1868 ; he retained his connection with this Presbytery until his death.   He received the honorary degree of Doctor of Divinity from Columbia College in 1852, and that of Doctor of Laws from Dartmouth College in 1868.

He was a Trustee of Hamilton College from 1867 until his death, and of Auburn Theological Seminary from 1872 to 1884, declining re-election.   He was also an Honorary Member of the American Board of Commissioners for Foreign Missions, a Life Director of the American Bible Society and of the American Tract Society, a member of the Oneida Historical Society, and of various other organizations with whose purposes he was in sympathy.   After his death the announcement was received of his election as an Honorary Member of the Northwestern Literary and Historical Society of Iowa.

He was married, February 10, 1846, to Mrs. Sarah (Van Vechten) Savage, widow of Professor Edward Savage, A.M., of Union College, and daughter of the Rev. Dr. Jacob and Catharine Van Wyck (Mason) Van Vechten, of Schenectady, N. Y., who survives him.   They had seven children, of whom five are still living.   He died in Utica, N. Y., November 4, 1885.

On Monday, November 2d, he returned to Utica from a month's visit in New York.   He had always enjoyed the life and movement of a great city, and this enjoyment was never more manifest than during these weeks.   He spent them chiefly in the companionship of his sister—who came to New York while he was there,—some of his children, and other near relatives ; taking the opportunity of greater leisure than had often fallen to his lot to make excursions to neighboring towns also, and renew old friendships. Those who were much with him in the course of these weeks remember the cheerful serenity of his bearing, the simple and tender directness of his affection, his quick sympathy, the breadth and geniality of his interest in all human affairs, the openness and expectancy of his mind toward questions which were occupying the thought of scholars, the gentle firmness of his opinions and judgments, his charity, and all the unassuming and even unconscious tokens of the hope which he had "as an anchor of the soul." These were not new qualities in him, but they seemed riper, and the whole life more rich and mellow than ever before. The beauty of the world was still a fresh delight to him. " I think I never had so *un*wearisome a ride from New York," he wrote, on reaching his journey's end, to one from whom he had that morning parted ; " with company nothing could have been more pleasant, even without, it was delightful. The sky and river, mountains and valley, were beautiful, till past Albany. Then we found snow, and the clouds again came about us, increasing in thickness till we reached Utica."— The unseen cloud was gathering fast over the heads of those that loved him.

It was afterward learned that when he left New York he had had a sense of oppression in the chest. He had felt it before, and was well aware that it might denote a serious affection of the heart. On Tuesday it had rather increased than diminished. This was the day of the State election, and he walked half a mile to deposit his ballots. In the course of the day he called upon his physician, who, after a thorough examination, recognized the gravity of the case, but hoped that the immediate danger might be averted. He returned to " The Waverly," which for four years had been to him and his family something like a home, spent the evening in writing letters and talking cheerfully with his wife and daughter, and retired at his usual hour. His sleep was fitful, and when, toward five o'clock in the morning of Wednesday, November 4th, he was asked if the night had not seemed long to him, he answered, quietly and gently, " Yes, rather long." A few minutes later, peacefully, without word or struggle, he ceased to breathe.

Funeral services were held in Utica, N. Y., on the morning of Friday, November 6th.

At " The Waverly " a few verses of Scripture were read, and prayer was offered by the Rev. Thomas J. Brown, D.D., Pastor of the Westminster Presbyterian Church of Utica ; after this, at half-past nine o'clock, the funeral procession moved to the church itself. The pall-bearers were the Hon. William J. Bacon, LL.D., William D. Walcott, Esq., Professor Edward North, L.H.D., the

Hon. Ellis H. Roberts, LL.D.—all of the Board of Trustees of Hamilton College, and Professor North a member of the Faculty, as well,—Professor C. H. F. Peters, Ph.D., of the Faculty, Dr. M. M. Bagg, Dr. John P. Gray, and the Hon. John F. Seymour. The Rev. Henry Darling, D.D., LL.D., President of Hamilton College, and all the remaining members of the Faculty, other members of the Board of Trustees, and a large company of kindred and friends gathered in the church.

As the procession entered the choir sang:

"Blessed are the dead that die in the Lord."

The Rev. Dr. Thomas J. Brown, Pastor, the Rev. Professor A. G. Hopkins, of Hamilton College, the Rev. Isaac S. Hartley, D.D., Pastor of the Reformed Church, Utica, and the Rev. Thomas B. Hudson, D.D., Pastor of the Presbyterian Church at Clinton, N. Y., occupied the pulpit.

Dr. T. J. Brown read, as the Scripture lesson, 1 Corinthians xv. 20–58; Dr. Hartley offered prayer; Dr. Hudson announced the hymn, which was sung by the choir:

"Sun of my soul, thou Saviour dear."

An address, full of delicate appreciation and sympathy, was delivered by Professor Hopkins.* At the close of the address Dr. T. J. Brown announced the hymn, which was sung by the choir:

"Asleep in Jesus! blessed sleep."

Prayer was then offered by the Pastor, who concluded the service with the benediction.

————

An urgent request came from the Faculty of Hamilton College, that the burial of Dr. BROWN might take place in the College Cemetery there. It seemed fitting, however, that he should be laid at rest with his kindred in the earlier home.

Funeral services were held at Hanover, N. H., on Sunday, November 8th, at two o'clock in the afternoon. From a house

* This address is printed in full on pp. 9 sqq.

whose doors, with most delicate and affectionate kindness, had been opened to receive his mortal remains, the casket was borne to the College Church by friends and former colleagues, this being their own desire.

The bearers were Elihu T. Quimby, A.M., formerly Professor of Mathematics in Dartmouth College ; the Hon. James W. Patterson, LL.D., formerly Professor of Mathematics and of Astronomy ; and Professors John K. Lord, A.M., John H. Wright, A.M., Charles F. Emerson, A.M., and Louis Pollens, A.M.

The church was filled with friends from the College and the village. In the pulpit were the Rev. Samuel C. Bartlett, D.D., LL.D., President of Dartmouth College, and the Rev. S. P. Leeds, D.D., Pastor of the College Church.

At the opening of the service the choir, consisting of Miss Sarah L. Smith, Mrs. F. A. Sherman, Mr. E. S. Hill, and Mr. C. L. Jenks, accompanied by Mr. G. W. Glass, organist, sang the hymn :

"Jesus, lover of my soul."

The Rev. Dr. Leeds read, as the Scripture lesson, John xiv. and other passages, and then announced the following hymn, which was sung by the choir :

"In vain our fancy strives to paint
    The moment after death,
The glories that surround the saint
    When he resigns his breath.

"One gentle sigh his fetters breaks ;
    We scarce can say, ' He's gone,'
Before the willing spirit takes
    Her mansion near the throne.

"Faith strives, but all its efforts fail,
    To trace her heavenward flight ;
No eye can pierce within the veil
    Which hides that world of light.

"Thus much (and this is all) we know,
    They are supremely blest ;
Have done with sin, and care, and woe,
    And with their Saviour rest."

A comprehensive and impressive address was then delivered by President Bartlett,* and was followed by a few tender and fitting remarks † from Dr. Leeds. President Bartlett then announced the following hymn, which was sung by the choir :

" Sleep thy last sleep !
   Free from care and sorrow ;
Rest, where none weep,
   Till th' eternal morrow :
Though dark waves roll
   O'er the silent river,
Thy fainting soul
   Jesus can deliver.

" Life's dream is past ;
   All its sin and sadness ;
Brightly at last
   Dawns the day of gladness.
Under thy sod,
   Earth, receive our treasure,
To rest in God !
   Waiting all his pleasure.

" Though we may mourn
   Those in life the dearest,
They shall return,
   Christ, when thou appearest !
Soon shall thy voice
   Comfort those now weeping,
Bidding rejoice
   All in Jesus sleeping."

The closing prayer was offered and the benediction pronounced by Dr. Leeds.

After the services in the church the interment took place in the village cemetery.

---

* This address is given in full, pp. 17 sqq.
† An abstract is given, pp. 22 sq.

I.

ADDRESS BY THE REV. PROFESSOR A. G. HOPKINS, OF HAMILTON COLLEGE,

WESTMINSTER CHURCH, UTICA, N. Y., NOVEMBER 6, 1885.

A GRACIOUS presence, a beloved companion and friend, has gone from us. Our lips are dumb, our hearts are torn with grief, and tears are the only response which we can make in this bewilderment of sorrow. The suddenness of the event has almost stunned us. It seems but yesterday that he was with us, on our streets, in our homes, apparently in the full tide of health,—the same genial greeting and friendly word, the same cheerfulness and hearty enjoyment in life and in work,—and with plans for an active future. Surely if any man seemed entitled to long life and length of days it was he, with a temper so gentle and even,—leading a life so quiet and unruffled, so full of peace within and peace without that there seemed no place for that friction which sometimes causes the delicate machinery of life to jar or to cease its action. These meetings and greetings— the refined and gentle face, the sunshine of his presence, the wisdom of his speech—are but memories now. In a moment, by an euthanasia which doubtless he himself would have chosen, that beautiful life was closed.

In a sermon which was preached by Dr. BROWN, in the Chapel of Hamilton College, on the death of Albert Barnes (after referring to Dr. Barnes' reunion with friends of college days in Philadelphia, Pa., in the summer of 1870), there occur these words :

"Scarcely five months had passed when one of the most noted of this group, apparently in quite his usual health and vigor, walked out of a Saturday to visit a friend, entered his house, sat down with an expression of fatigue or slight distress, and instantly, as we may say, was forever at rest. A very touching petition in the Litany is the prayer that we may be delivered from sudden death, *i.e.*, says one writer, from death for which we are not prepared. Were the steps of that good man specially ordered as he breasted the strong, cold wind, and so induced that overaction which was too much for a frame less vigorous than it seemed? Perhaps it was even so ; and his prayer was answered that some disease ' not tardy to perform its destined office, yet with gentle stroke,' might remove him ; and he was mercifully spared the suffering and anticipation of death which it is said he feared. To his family and friends the shock was of course terrible ; but with him that immediate and painless transition must have been of the nature of a glorious surprise. His lips were hardly silent upon earth before he caught the language of another world."

Were these words written by Dr. BROWN in unconscious anticipation of the kind of death which he himself thought most desirable and happy ? In writing afterward of Dr. Barnes' death he speaks of it as " a life so suddenly ended, I think I may say so happily ended." With slight change of circumstances and with change of name Dr. BROWN has described in these words, written fifteen years ago, his own sudden and painless death. A return from a pleasant visit with his children, a happy reunion with his family, a slight sense of uneasiness without positive distress or pain, a night of rest, a question toward daybreak, and, without time even to hear the reply, his spirit had departed. Verily to him, as to Dr. Barnes, " that immediate and painless transition must have been of the nature of a glorious surprise." What constitutes to us perhaps a large part of the bitterness of our grief was certainly to him the happiest feature of his release. He has gone upon a journey which he had long and calmly contemplated, and of which I believe he had no dread. In the graces of his Christian character he had beautifully ripened into fitness for that change, and in the last moments of his life his heart was unruffled. By a blessed transformation, which, I am sure, we all might envy him, in a moment " he was not, for God had taken him." We grieve that he was instantly cut off, in the maturity of his powers—when the judgment was never so sound, when the heart throbbed with tenderest affections ; when the mind in full vigor was gathering its ample forces for new excursions in the realm of letters. Is it not rather an occasion for gratitude that, after a career of great usefulness and honor, he passed peacefully to his reward in the full possession of his powers ?

In that memorable discourse which Dr. BROWN delivered in this pulpit, on the 8th of February, 1874, on the character and the public services of Dr. Fisher, he recited briefly, and in language which none but he could command, the touching and pathetic story of the closing years of the life of that distinguished man, his own predecessor in the Presidency of Hamilton College. " The darkened understanding (I quote from that discourse) emerged again into the light—or rather into a dim, unchangeable twilight. The weeks and months as they passed brought no return of the thick darkness, but neither did they bring the clear day. It became evident after a while that the work of that busy and overwrought brain was done ; that no more burdens could be laid upon it, no more tasks accomplished." Are we wrong in counting those happy who fall even with armor on and equipped for further usefulness, as compared with the death in life of a shattered and darkened intellect ? Are we wrong, in view of the possible infirmities of advancing age, when we count our friend happy in the time and manner of his death ? A beautiful life had been well rounded out ; a life abounding in pure and gracious influences was moving on toward the inevitable infirmities of age ; an eminently useful and permanent work had been accomplished. There is an element of mercy even in these bitter experiences of life, and though the sorrows which we suffer seem the heaviest of all, yet God is good as well as wise when He does not leave to us the ordering of our days.

This is not the place for, nor does time admit, any detailed analysis of Dr. BROWN'S character. Indeed, his development was so symmetrical that it is impossible to seize upon this or that trait as pre-eminently characteristic. There was a fulness and completeness in his composition. Birth and inheritance had done much for him; contact in life and letters with noble minds had added a rare refinement to his life; and to this was added the crowning glory of a truly Christian spirit. Indeed, there must have been a happy combination of inherited and acquired gifts, of graces of mind and of heart, to produce this singularly gracious, scholarly, and cultivated man. Those who knew him best were often in doubt as to what they most admired in him; whether it were his qualities of heart or of mind; whether it were the genial and affectionate companion or the learned and scholarly man. But certainly in him mind and heart had combined to produce that rare but beautiful flower of our civilization—a thoroughly cultivated Christian gentleman.

No one could see much of Dr. BROWN without being impressed with the amiableness and gentleness of his character. Every bitter ingredient seemed omitted from his composition. Nor was this merely the result of broad culture, which ofttimes smoothes away the sharp edges of life and gives even to rough natures a philosophic calm. The foundation of these qualities in him was a good heart. Goodness, charity, a broad sympathy with men were ruling features in his life. He was utterly incapable of narrow prejudice or bitter enmity. Though his opinions were clearly defined, and his convictions positive, he was neither by nature nor practice a controversialist. He had no fondness for the strife of words. In the quiet and affection of the home circle, or in the society of friends, his genial nature found contentment and rest. He was generous and warm in his attachments; there was nothing cautious or calculating in his friendships. This gentleness, or Christian self-control, manifested itself in all the relations of life. Though passing most of his life as an instructor, a career in which there may be danger of developing dogmatic tendencies, he was uniformly courteous and tolerant toward the opinions of others, a courtesy and tolerance which were perhaps in part the fruit of his wide knowledge of letters and men. The bitter speech, the sharp retort, though doubtless sometimes deserved, were never heard from him. Those who knew him well and saw him much, even in times of trial and provocation, affirm that he never was betrayed into speech or conduct which could wound the feelings of another, or which could occasion himself regret. These qualities of mind and heart, too rare in our age, we do well to emphasize and emulate. Kindred with this was a love of truth, an open, manly directness in speech and action which won the confidence and respect of all. No one ever doubted or impugned his motives. He was utterly devoid of artifice. His utterance was fortified by his character, and carried with it all the weight of an earnest Christian life.

His sympathies in the world of art were as broad as his sympathies with men. No branch of learning was beneath or beyond the range of his interest. His love and perception of the beautiful were naturally keen and delicate, and that love had been strengthened and cultivated by study, by travel, and by intercourse with art in its varied forms. His love of nature was also marked. He saw her beauties and drew lessons from her various forms which were full of wisdom and instruction. All of these things indicate a nature many-sided, with manifold avenues open to the outer world. He received the message of science, of letters, of art, and he sent it out again to eager, inquiring minds clothed in the beautiful or the stately garb of an English prose which was the delight and the despair of all who listened.

But wide as were his sympathies and broad as was his learning, Dr. BROWN'S pre-eminence doubtless was as a

man of letters. His familiarity with all that was best in
literature of the past and present was wide and varied.
His excursions in these fields were delightful and instructive. No one who has ever heard his lectures upon the
English statesmen, or orators, or poets, can ever forget the
charm of that pen or the enjoyment of that hour. In his
hands the English language was an instrument of wonderful flexibility and power. He had sounded its depths
and tested its strength as few men of this generation have
done.

To listen to those wonderful discourses upon Pitt, or
Burke, or Fox, or to tread with him the path of English
letters from Chaucer down through the centuries, was a revelation of the power, richness, and beauty of our English
speech. His array of facts was masterly, his presentation
of the subject exhaustive, while over all he threw that
marvellous grace of speech which made all his discourses
models of chaste and elegant composition. He turned his
pen to many different kinds of composition, and with simple truth we say of him : " He touched no subject which
he did not adorn." His sermons, whether delivered in the
College Chapel or on occasions of public interest, were always rich in thought, stimulating in their spiritual tone, and
elegant in form. For a young man to have heard his discourses, at intervals, during a period of four years, was
almost a liberal education.

In the more difficult field of metaphysical inquiry, his
studies were equally thorough, his discourses equally instructive and luminous. His mind seemed admirably fitted to
deal with the abstract ideas and subtle distinctions of mental
science. When following his guidance here, one argued that
he should never leave the chair of the instructor ; when
hearing his admirable discourses, one was equally convinced
that his sphere was pre-eminently the pulpit and the platform. In all his public addresses he was singularly happy.
Such discourses as those already referred to—on Dr.
Barnes and Dr. Fisher, or the later one on the life of Mr.

Marsh—were received with universal favor, and two of them at least he was called upon to repeat on several different occasions. His delicate sense of propriety, and of what was suitable to time and place, led him always to say what seemed exactly the right thing, so that one who knew and admired him said: "Dr. BROWN never makes a mistake." It is possible, as has been said, that the highest honor of his life came to him with the Presidency of Hamilton College. Yet he bore his honors so quietly that apparently no station seemed too high, nor any useful station too low. For fifteen years he adorned that honorable position by his virtues and his learning. He has left the impress of his life and character upon all who knew him. During that period five hundred young men shared his instruction and were moulded, to some degree, by his influence. As a citizen, as a neighbor, as a colleague, his name in yonder little village and in that institution of learning will be held in honored and loving remembrance. He has left his monument in human hearts, more enduring than any sculptured column. Our poor words can do him no honor. The truest tribute to his memory would be to imitate his virtues ; to reproduce the gentleness of his life, its sterling integrity, its Christian meekness, and to try to diffuse through the life which is about us those gracious elements of character which we have admired in our departed friend.

And to you, my Christian friends, I need surely speak no word of counsel or of comfort. You were the members of his household. The faith which he shared was your faith also. The blessed hopes of immortality which he indulged are also yours. What we vaguely speak of as the other world, as friend after friend departs, comes finally to be the world in which our thoughts tarry with the greatest interest. That world is no other world to him. It is the world in which much of his life had been spent ; the world of spiritual influence, of pure thought, of useful and innocent activities, of holy desires, of service to God and to man. You have all the consolations which may come from the memory of a good life usefully spent and peacefully ended in the hopes of a glorious immortality.

It certainly was a blessed privilege, and one hardly to be expected, that so many of you should have seen his face and enjoyed his presence so shortly before his death. Had a kind Heavenly Father graciously ministered to your desire in this regard, as perhaps He did, you could hardly have asked for more at His hands. He has gone to no strange country. Surely there were beckoning hands and loving voices on that other shore to give him greeting. Let us not mourn our pious and sainted dead as though some great calamity had befallen them. What he said of another was doubtless true of him : "Hardly had his ear lost the accents of this world when it caught the language of another world." His memory, his virtues, his Christian character are your priceless legacy.

> " His life was gentle ; and the elements
> So mixed in him that Nature might stand up,
> And say to all the world, ' This was a man ! ' "

II.

ADDRESS BY THE REV. S. C. BARTLETT, D.D., LL.D., PRESIDENT OF DARTMOUTH COLLEGE,

IN THE COLLEGE CHURCH, HANOVER, N. H., NOVEMBER 8, 1885.

WE have come hither to pay our tribute of respect to a well-rounded character, a long, useful, and honored life, and to a history closely, not to say centrally, related to Dartmouth College.

Eighty-four years ago Francis Brown,* the father of SAMUEL GILMAN BROWN, came as a student to this institution; and during somewhat more than half the time that has since elapsed some member of that family has been here as student, Professor, or President—indeed, jointly and separately, for more than half a century. The father, raised up by a good Providence for a special work, ten years after his graduation was elected President of the institution in the critical time of its history, and went through the stormy struggle with the Legislature and the Judiciary of New Hampshire for the chartered rights and existence of the College. A man of singular attractiveness of spirit and of remarkable skill and ability, he accomplished his trying task, but sank under its terrible burden and strain. He saved the College, and lost his life. His wife survived for many years, to train her son in his father's ways and

---

* See Appendix II.

2

traits, and to witness, in her old age, his well-earned honors. Some of us here remember her well, and her rare excellence of mind and manner, of heart and life.*

The child of such a noble parentage, SAMUEL GILMAN BROWN came to this place a boy two years of age. Here he completed his College course at the age of eighteen. Hither, nine years later, he returned to be for twenty-seven consecutive years in the Professor's chair. After some fourteen years in the Presidency of Hamilton College, hither he returned to give us two more years of his pleasant society and ripened experience as an instructor ; and nearly if not quite the last of his correspondence was directed to this place, and concerned the College that he loved so well. Here, continuously or at intervals, for nearly seventy years his face and form were a familiar sight ; here his hospitable mansion was for more than a quarter of a century an attractive resort ; here he formed and maintained life-long, unbroken friendships ; here he gained a wide circle of literary acquaintance, and established an enviable reputation ; and here more than fifteen hundred graduates passed under his moulding hand. To this place he always turned with an enthusiasm that grew with his advancing years. He dwelt, in his later days, upon this scenery around us with more than youthful delight ; and so deep-seated was his interest in this, his childhood's and manhood's home, that he said he loved the very stones in its streets. To this place he longingly looked as the home of his declining years, and here to-day he finds his last resting-place on earth.

Dr. BROWN'S life was connected with some of the best days and best men that the College has ever seen. He was associated with those two men, rare in their different ways, alike in fervor of piety, Presidents Lord and Smith—the one massive in character, deep and speculative in thought, the other active, enterprising, versatile, and genial ; with the ourtly and accomplished Haddock, of Websterian blood

---

* See Appendix III.

and reserved power ; with the earnest and clean-cut mathe-
matician Chase ; with Long, that acutest of metaphysicians
and kindliest of men ; with Alpheus Crosby, unsurpassed in
the country, in his day, for his knowledge of the Greek language and literature ; with Putnam, model of all that was
lovely in spirit, and broad and high in culture ; with Young,
the admirable father and his distinguished son ; and with other
men of like intellect and power, still among the living, whom
therefore I will not mention, except to speak of the ency-
clopædic Sanborn, then robust and stimulating, now tot-
tering on the utmost verge of life. These were the men
with whom he found his sympathetic sphere of literary
labor.

Dr. BROWN's literary productiveness commenced soon
after the close of his theological studies at Andover Seminary. A review of the great preacher, Thomas Chalmers, in
the " Biblical Repository," first displayed to the public the
drift of his character, the clearness of his discernment, and
the vigor of his style. At the age of twenty-four he was a
man of mark, and three years later he was installed in the
Professor's chair.

To follow his long and successful career this is not the
time or place. The best indications alike of his own instinc-
tive sympathies and of the general estimate of his literary
qualities may be found in the fact that he was the man
selected to edit the works and write the life of that eminent
genius, Rufus Choate ; to deliver the Historical Oration of
Dartmouth College at its hundredth anniversary ; to pro-
nounce before the Alumni at Chicago the centennial birth-
day discourse on the great statesman, Daniel Webster ; and,
again, to give the Memorial Address and write the life of
that distinguished scholar, George Perkins Marsh. These
are specimens. The full details of his literary labors—
Lowell Lectures, public orations, sermons in many a pulpit, essays, baccalaureates, lectures in the class-room, faithful services in the Presidency at Hamilton College, and
the unfinished literary task of his closing days—must be

written by some loving hand as skilful in characterization as his own.

It might seem presumptuous in me, though I had been brought in contact with Dr. BROWN at times for more than forty years, to attempt even an outline of his character in the presence of those who have known him so much more intimately. But to me he seemed a Puritan without asceticism or ostentation, a scholar of broad and cultivated taste, a companion both thoughtful and playful, an observer of men both watchful and kind, a man self-poised and self-contained, without repulsions, and of spirit cheerful and hopeful, a friend of many and an enemy of none. Of his life in the home circle it does not become me to speak. Notably enough, one of the last acts of his life was an act of twofold filial affection. Less than forty hours before his death I received from him a letter completing the arrangement for a memorial window to his honored father in the new Chapel of his beloved Alma Mater.

Indeed, I know not how I can more clearly set before you the inner spirit and outer exhibition of the man, the scholar, the thinker, and the Christian teacher, than as exemplified in one of his ardent utterances at that centennial of the College. Shall I read those weighty sentences, hard by the place where they were uttered, and before the silent tongue that uttered them shall have passed away from this house where so often it has been heard ? After his rapid sketch of the history of the College, and before his clear characterization of the intellectual breadth and vigorous mental gymnastics of the curriculum on which such a body of Alumni have been trained to their manly work, he thus utters himself on its great central force :

" As the motto on its [the College's] seal indicated and expressed the religious purpose of its founders, so this purpose never has been lost sight of. Through lustrum after lustrum and generation after generation, while classes have succeeded classes, while one corps of instructors have passed away and others have taken their places, the high purpose of presenting and enforcing the vital and essential truths of the Christian religion has never been forgotten or neglected. The power of Christianity in modifying, inspiring, and directing the energies of modern civilization—its art, its literature, its commerce, its laws, and its government—has been profoundly felt. Nor has it been for a moment forgotten that education, to be truly and in the largest sense beneficent, must also be religious ; must affect that which is deepest in man ; must lead him, if it can, to the contemplation of truths most personal, central, and essential ; must open to him some of those depths where the soul swings almost helplessly in the midst of experiences and powers unfathomable and infinite, where the intellect falters and hesitates, and finds no solution till it yields to faith. Within later years there have been those who have advocated the doctrine that education should be entirely secular, that the college should have nothing to do with religious counsels or advice. Now, while I do not think this would be easy, as our colleges are organized, without leaving or even inciting the mind to dangerous scepticism, nor without depriving the soul of that food which it specially craves, and destitute of which it will grow lean, hungry, and unsatisfied,—as matter of history no such theory of education has found favorable response among the guardians of Dartmouth."

So spake out once more the old Puritan soul of Eleazar Wheelock, and the resolute heart of Francis Brown, through the lips now sealed in death. So rang out loud and clear the key-note of the College for the second century, to reverberate in the ears of its guardians, teachers, and students for all coming time. And so, "being dead, he yet speaketh" words of the century and for the centuries.

And now from the scenes where he faithfully labored so long, enjoyed so much, and drew around him so many cords of interest and affection, we shall tenderly take up our departed friend—this cultivated scholar, experienced teacher, finished writer, impressive preacher, courteous gentleman, genial companion, and steadfast Christian—and shall carry him to another spot near by, not unfamiliar to his thoughts and his footsteps, thickly thronged, as he was wont to say, with precious dust, and, by the side of his father and his mother, his brother and his children, not far from a cluster of lovely and beloved relatives, and surrounded by many a friend who knew and loved him well, we shall lay him down till the heavens be no more.

III.

REMARKS BY THE REV. S. P. LEEDS, D.D.,

In the College Church, Hanover, N. H., November 8, 1885.

[The remarks of Dr. Leeds were unwritten, and the following sentences are based upon notes, taken as he spoke, by one who was kind enough to attempt this difficult service.]

Two pictures present themselves to me : one, of a little boy coming here seventy years ago with his father ; the other, of a man approaching old age, returning here in the November of life, before the winter's snow had appeared. Between these are two others, one showing him in his prime, not yet fifty, active amid his associates—Professor Long, a few years older than he ; Professor Noyes, fourteen months his senior ; Professor Hubbard, about his own age ; and then the younger Professors—Patterson and Fairbanks, Putnam, whom he so much loved ; Aiken, Packard, and Varney. In the other picture he is at home in his parlor, so genial and courteous, or in a little room beyond, with his family and a few others, assembled by an open fire, happy, appreciative of his friends, and beloved by them. . . . I think of him as a man who had had a wise, steady-handed, good mother. His father was taken from him when he was a child. The wisdom and grace of the mother passed into the son. . . . He was extremely careful not to utter criticism. He would defend others from it. His extreme tenderness was very noticeable ; as expressed by one to whom he was as kind as a brother, it was "an unutterable tenderness." . . . In his later years I was impressed with his love of the past and his interest in the future. He was sensitive to change, yet he kept up fully with the present. Every old tree he was fond of; every object with which he was familiar he was fond of, and yet how interested he was in the present. In his last visit to this village I was struck with his interest in all its changes and improvements, and almost every change seemed to him an improvement. He loved the present, he took pleasure in the society of men; to a remarkable degree he enjoyed the present life without selfishness, illustrating how a good man may enjoy.

That he was a Christian man we all knew. . . . Of late I was impressed with the deepening Christian spirit and influence manifest in him, an example of a true Christian experience, of one that had been enriched by the Spirit of God. [Here followed a short account of the close of his life.]

We have come to-day as Christians to speak of a Christian. We recall a long career, and a useful one; as the Professor who fills the chair he used to fill expressed it to me the other day, "a splendid career." But best of all is that he was a follower of Christ. We have not met as unbelievers; we rejoice for one who has finished his course in the love of Jesus Christ; we sorrow, too, with those who are Christians and have Christian hopes. He has gone away from us, but he has not gone into a strange place. *We* are in the strange place. He is not an exile; *we* are the exiles. We must wait yet a little longer; he has gone where he will be forever with the Lord.

IV.

REMARKS BY THE REV. PROFESSOR HENRY L. CHAPMAN, A.M., OF BOWDOIN COLLEGE,

IN THE COLLEGE CHAPEL, BRUNSWICK, ME., SUNDAY EVENING, NOVEMBER 8, 1885.

[These remarks were published in *The Bowdoin Orient* of November 11, 1885, with the following words prefixed: "It was with deep and sincere regret that we learned of the death of Professor SAMUEL G. BROWN, D.D., upon the 4th of November. During the two years of his Professorship at Bowdoin he won many friends by his kindly interest and unostentatious devotion to duty, and when he left, last Commencement, he bore with him the respect and love of the students."]

WITHIN these few days we have received intelligence of the death of one whom many of us have had reason to regard with sincere respect and affection, and whose death touches us with a sense of personal loss. It seems fitting that in this place, where he has so often led our Sabbath-evening devotions, joining with us in our hymns of praise, and presenting our common needs and aspirations at the throne of grace—it seems fitting that we should devote a few moments this evening to the grateful remembrance of his association with us, and to the recognition of his personal virtues and of his services to the college.

Dr. BROWN, as you know, was not a graduate of this College, and the service to which he was called here was understood from the first to be a temporary service. It is with special feelings of gratitude, therefore, that we may recall his varied and unselfish labors in behalf of all the interests of the College. He could not have exhibited more genuine solicitude for the welfare of his own Alma Mater than he exhibited for that of the College which called him to a brief service in the very evening of his days. Without abating, so far as could be seen, one jot of the loyalty that he owed to other institutions with which he had been more closely connected, he nevertheless espoused the interests of this institution with a generosity and heartiness that could not fail to win our affectionate regard.

Not content, as many might have been in similar circumstances, with performing, however faithfully, the duties of his department of instruction, he was always ready to do what lay in his power to further the general interests of the College, and to contribute what was always a most important and delightful element to the social and intellectual life of our little community.

Those who enjoyed the benefit of his regular instructions have gone out from among us; but we who remain will certainly bear willing witness to the value of his thoughtful and manly discourses in the pulpit, of his stimulating and eloquent lectures before the Literary Association, of his earnest and reverent ministrations at this desk. By these labors of love, wrought with a cheerfulness that added to their charm, he made us all his debtors, and the remembrance of the debt renews our reverence for his memory.

It may well give us satisfaction also to know, from his own hand, that his residence among us was a source of pleasure to himself as well as to us. In a letter received from him shortly after his departure, a letter filled with the kindliness which always characterized his intercourse with others, he uses these words, which it is a pleasure to repeat in this presence: " In all my experience of college life I cannot recall any two years which have passed more agreeably, with classes more diligent and faithful, or with less to interrupt the steadfast and constant labors of the department. I shall always recall those classes with affectionate interest."

And these very words give us a glimpse of one of the

winning characteristics of our departed friend. He was quick to perceive what was good in those about him. It is the mark of a generous and a Christian spirit. A selfish and suspicious nature misses the good in its eagerness to detect the weakness and the wickedness of men. But Dr. BROWN was eager to respond to every sign of friendliness, of courtesy, of faithful effort, and of personal worthiness in those with whom he came in contact. The breadth and fineness of his culture did not separate him from men, but gave a certain graciousness to his intercourse with them, which is the most attractive fruit of culture.

With a heart that never seemed to feel the touch of age, with sympathies that broadened as his years increased, with tastes that were sensitive to every form of beauty, powers that were consecrated to the service of truth, and affections that were fixed unchangeably upon the good,— he went in and out among us for two brief years, respected and beloved, and has now passed beyond all earthly associations. His work was done. He had passed a most honored and useful life, and was ready to hear the sentence, the anticipation of which robs death of all its terror, "Well done, good and faithful servant." "Above all," says Lord Bacon, "believe me, the sweetest canticle is 'Nunc dimittis,' when a man hath obtained worthy ends and expectations."

And let us receive this lesson of God's providence, of our own mortality, and of the opportunities of human life, with reasonable and reverent minds, and in the exercise of a humble faith.

Directly in the respective pathways we are following, somewhere in the uncertain future, lies the shadow of death, into which we shall enter and straightway be lost to earthly eyes. Every returning Sabbath, every setting sun, nay, every fleeting breath, brings us nearer to that shadow. Shall we enter it to-night, or to-morrow, or after many days? Will it be in the spring-time, when nature is waking to new life, or in autumn, when the fading leaf teaches us the lesson of our mortality? Will it be this year, or next, or are there many years to come, each laden for us with its pleasures and its cares?

Certainly no one can answer these questions, nor need we greatly care to answer them. There are other questions of graver import that press upon us. Is that shadow something to shrink from and to fear? Is it the end of our being and all our hopes? Are we really lost when we enter it? Is it the great misfortune of our lives, which, as long as possible, we are to avoid at whatever cost of other things, and to yield to, at the last, in utter despair?

There is an answer to these questions. The revelation of our Lord Jesus Christ, to him who will receive it, makes that shadow as harmless, and as little to be feared, as the mist that closes around one who climbs some high mountain in the assured faith that he will find sunlight at the top.

We may live, as he of whom we have been thinking lived, in the light and comfort of that revelation, doing our work humbly and faithfully as good stewards of the manifold grace of God. Like him, realizing the familiar and beautiful words of one of our own poets, we may

> " So live, that when our summons comes to join
> The innumerable caravan that moves
> To that mysterious realm, where each shall take
> His chamber in the silent halls of death,
> We go not, like the quarry-slave at night,
> Scourged to his dungeon, but sustained and soothed
> By an unfaltering trust approach the grave,
> Like one who wraps the drapery of his couch
> About him, and lies down to pleasant dreams."

V.

OBITUARY NOTICE BY THE REV. PROFESSOR HENRY E. PARKER, D.D., OF DARTMOUTH COLLEGE.

———

[At the regular meeting for conference and prayer, held in Hanover, Sunday evening, November 8th, Professor Parker paid a tribute to the memory of Dr. BROWN. The following notice was published in *The Dartmouth*, November 13, 1885 :]

DIED suddenly, from affection of the heart, in Utica, N. Y., Wednesday, November 4th, SAMUEL GILMAN BROWN, D.D., LL.D. Thus has passed away another of our illustrious Alumni, and one who was long and most honorably connected with the Faculty of the College. Born in 1813, at North Yarmouth, Me., he graduated at the early age of eighteen in the Class of 1831. He studied divinity at the Theological Seminary, Andover, Mass., graduating from there in 1837. Two years subsequently were spent in foreign travel, when he returned to his Alma Mater to assume the duties of the Chair of Oratory and Belles-Lettres. This Professorship he successfully filled for twenty-three years, when he was transferred to the Professorship of Intellectual Philosophy and Political Economy. After filling this Chair also successfully for four years he was elected to the Presidency of Hamilton College, which office he filled for fourteen years, resigning in 1881. He afterward, for a while, filled his former Chair here, then vacant, and subsequently a similar position at Bowdoin.

Dr. SAMUEL G. BROWN was the son of the Rev. Dr.

Francis Brown, third President of the College, a man of rare endowments of person, mind, and character. Called to the administration of the College at a most critical period in its history, when its very existence was pending upon the decisions of the Courts, he filled a peculiarly arduous position with great efficiency, acceptableness, and success, but with the sacrifice of his valuable life, for he died at thirty-six, the year following the decision of the United States Supreme Court in favor of the College.

The son repeated the father's superior and agreeable traits ; and though but a boy of seven at his father's premature decease, he continued to have the nurture and guidance of a mother of rare wisdom and worth. He grew up to a beautiful manhood. Of handsome face and form, dignified and engaging, affable and most courteous, mind and character corresponded to all that was externally attractive. Admirably filling all home relations, of son and brother, husband and father, he was the faithful associate, the warmhearted friend, the genial, delightful companion. A devotee of books, his reading was very extensive, choice, and available. He had a mind exceedingly well disciplined and stored. His voice, which as an instructor in oratory he had cultivated with especial care, was unusually rich in its tones and of wide and varied compass. His style of speaking was finished and effective. His style of writing, too, was classic in its beauty. He wrote much and he wrote well— lectures, discourses, addresses, essays, and reviews. His biography of Rufus Choate gained him a wide and deserved reputation. He leaves unfinished a biography of the late George P. Marsh, upon which he was engaged.

The society of Dr. BROWN was very pleasant as it was improving ; his intelligence made it so, with his cordial ways, his animation of feature thought, and voice, his high-mindedness, freshness, and freedom from commonplace. Culture marked his thoughts, his expressions, his tones and manner, with now and then a delightful spicing of pleasantry and quiet fun, with never a shade of bitterness or malevolence.   He was a good *raconteur*.   He heartily enjoyed a good thing said or told by another, and seldom failed to match it by something as good of his own. But everywhere and always he was the Christian gentle-man.   Indeed, religious principle characterized all that he was and did.   He was a sturdy champion of what he be-lieved to be the true and the right, and it would be difficult to find an instance of his swerving from their practical ex-emplification.   It was this which perfected the grace and finish of what he was.   He loved religious observances. He loved Christian words and ways.   It was his genuine and living piety, with its inward and outward blossoming and fruitage, which made so sweet and redolent and valu-able that life now hidden from our eyes, but never to be forgotten.   One who has known him long and well, early enough to be his pupil, and late enough to have been as-sociated with him in instruction, may be permitted fervently to speak of a character and life of such rare symmetry and beauty, where there seemed so little lacking and nothing in disproportionate excess.   His very death seemed con-sonant and fitting—no wasting, suffering illness—nothing but the simple, peaceful transferrence from this life to the next.   And such a death was his own desire.   It reminds us of Dr. Jeremy Belknap, the historian of New Hampshire, whose similar wish was similarly gratified, and among whose papers, after his decease, were found the following lines :

> " When faith and patience, hope and love,
> Have made us meet for heaven above,
> How blest the privilege to rise,
> Snatched in a moment to the skies ;
> Unconscious to resign our breath,
> Nor taste the bitterness of death."

VI.

MEMORIAL PRESENTED BY THE HON. WILL-IAM J. BACON, LL.D., OF UTICA, N. Y.,

To the Board of Trustees of Hamilton College, Clinton, N. Y., November 17, 1885.

———

As we come together again after the annual convocation in July last, we naturally look around us to recognize and to greet those from whom we then separated, and at once we realize with a sad certainty that there is here a vacant chair. It was occupied by one we always met with a cheerful look and a loving word. In the felicitous language of another on the occasion of his funeral obsequies, "a gracious presence, a beloved companion, has gone from us, and our lips are dumb, our hearts torn with anguish."

Samuel Gilman Brown, D.D., ex-President of Hamilton College, suddenly departed this life in the early hours of the morning of November 4, 1885. The event was entirely unlooked for, and our whole community was startled as by an electric shock. All who knew him felt that a great and good man had gone from us, and the mortal had by an instantaneous transition "put on immortality." To us who were so intimately and happily associated with him, the loss of his pleasant companionship, his benignant manner, his gentle courtesy, his wise and conservative counsels can hardly be expressed, while it is profoundly felt.

We do not propose to dwell at any length upon the incidents of his public career, on the special and attractive features of the life he lived among his friends, and those which pre-eminently marked that life in the sacred precincts of that home which was to him the very centre of his being, the place where he had garnered up his heart, and upon which he shed the radiance of perpetual sunshine. These have to some extent been already publicly and most appropriately noticed, and doubtless will be hereafter more fully and amply commemorated.

It will be enough here to say that he was born at North Yarmouth, in Maine, on January 4, 1813 ; that he graduated at Dartmouth College, of which his distinguished father, Dr. Francis Brown, was President, and subsequently from the Theological Seminary at Andover ; that he travelled somewhat extensively in Europe from 1838 to 1840, and returning home was almost immediately engaged in instruction at Dartmouth, first in the department of Oratory, and subsequently as Professor of Intellectual Philosophy. From this position he was called, in 1866, to the Presidency of Hamilton College, in which office, with conspicuous ability, he remained until his resignation in 1881. Since that date he has made his home in Utica, but has been engaged for portions of three years in giving instruction both in intellectual and moral philosophy at Dartmouth and at Bowdoin Colleges, and in other literary labors. At the time of his death he was gathering materials for what would doubtless have been his crowning, as it was to him a most congenial, work, the life of that learned scholar and eminent statesman, George P. Marsh, of Vermont.

Dr. BROWN was a scholar of wide and varied attainments, and enjoyed a large reputation as a master of that mother tongue that seems to us the most happy and appropriate vehicle for pure and lofty thought, and strong as well as polished diction. He was familiar with the whole range of English literature, from its crudest, roughest elements and uncouth forms in Chaucer and Gower to the latest and most refined and polished numbers of Tennyson and the masculine and magnificent periods of Macaulay. His own style was formed upon the highest models, and was distinguished in his public addresses no less by clearness and elevation of thought than a peculiar felicity of diction that left nothing uncompleted or unfinished. Of him as truly as of

Goldsmith it could be said : " *Nihil tetigit quod non ornavit.*"

The transparent beauty as well as the strength of his thought, and the almost unmatched perfection of his style, appeared to great advantage in his addresses to the graduating classes in the college, and those other discourses delivered on several memorable occasions, and notably those at the service commemorative of President Fisher, and the memorial address on the life and public career of George P. Marsh.

In his pulpit discourses the same finish of style appeared, applied to themes inspired by profound thought and deep and holy meditation. We have the authority of one well qualified to judge, and whose opportunities of hearing him from the pulpit as well as the platform were most frequent and favorable, for saying, as we do in his own appreciative words : " His sermons, whether delivered in the College Chapel or on occasions of public interest, were always rich in thought, stimulating in their spiritual tone, and finished in form. For a young man to have heard his discourses at intervals during a period of four years was almost of itself a liberal education."

Of the private character and personal traits of Dr. BROWN, it is difficult to speak without using terms that may seem to border at least upon extravagant eulogium. But surely it may be truthfully said that no one who enjoyed the inestimable privilege of his friendship could be brought into close communion with him without a profound and lasting impression of the purity and elevation of his character, the extent and thoroughness of his culture, and a wonderful increment of deep admiration and reverent love for the daily beauty of the life that diffused while it received so much of genuine enjoyment. His natural temperament was serene as well as buoyant, and he had so disciplined both his intellect and his heart that he had acquired an absolute self-control that manifested itself even amid circumstances of great trial and provocation. No one to whom he had given

3

his confidence had any reason to fear its withdrawal save by his own ill desert, and so frank and ingenuous was his nature that having no disguise himself he was very slow to suspect its existence in others.

It was most fitting that a life so gentle, so symmetrical, so complete, should have an ending so beautiful that it hardly calls forth any emotions save those of holy joy and sincere congratulation. He was apparently in good health, and to the outward eye his physical condition exhibited no sign of the hidden foe that was making, all unseen, his stealthy approaches toward the citadel of life. He was in full possession of all his fine powers and attainments. He felt comparatively little of the infirmities that commonly attend advancing years or the decrepitude of coming age. He was most mercifully spared months or even weeks of racking pain, or the solemn and sometimes disturbing apprehensions that not infrequently are the precursors of approaching dissolution. He had no occasion to bid "fond nature cease her strife" and let him "languish into life," the life upon whose inner verge he doubtless unconsciously stood.

With the composure of one that lies down to quiet dreams, with a comparatively short season of previous bodily suffering, without a struggle or a sigh, he gently yielded his soul to his Creator, and literally "fell on sleep." And thus it was that with a bound his emancipated spirit, dropping the fleshly tabernacle that held it, passed from the side of the dearest companionship of earth to the immediate presence of the Father whom he reverently adored, and the Saviour whom he wholly trusted and supremely loved, and so in a moment he was translated, and was "forever with the Lord." Who would not be happy to have lived such a life—who is there that envies not such a death?

> " Of no contagion, of no blast, he died,
>   But fell like autumn fruit that mellowed long.
>   So freshly he ran on three score and ten,
>   And then the busy wheels of life stood still."

VII.

REMARKS BY THE REV. THOMAS J. BROWN, D.D.,

In the Westminster Presbyterian Church, Utica, N. Y., January 3, 1886.

[The Communion Sunday following Dr. Brown's Death.]

WHETHER or not our custom is a wise one of coupling with the commemoration of our Lord's death mention of our own dear ones who have died I do not know, but this is true, that easily and almost inevitably the thought of His death sets us thinking, too, of those who have died in Him. All our hope for them, the hope for ourselves that we may see them again and know them, centres in Him. If we are to "sorrow not as others who have no hope," it must be by our believing "that as Jesus died and rose again, even so them also which sleep in Jesus will God bring with Him." Moreover, our thoughts of them as they now are, indistinct at best, all associate them with Him, where He is. "*With the Lord*" is the best account we can give, even to our own hearts, of their present state and station. Whatever is uncertain, of this we are confident, that in their behalf is fulfilled His prayer, "Father, I will that they also whom thou hast given me be with me where I am." How, then, shall we think of Him and not of them? Nor need we fear lest He should be offended at this—offended if even as we sit at this table, in holy contemplation of our Lord, there

rise also before us these other familiar forms, not inter-
vening between Him and us, but so associated with Him
that, we cannot think of them apart.   We fully appreciate
that, "with the Lord" and "beholding His glory," they
already have experiences of which we cannot form even a
conception ; but their hearts we know have not changed.
They are the same to us that they ever were.   No height
or depth of experience, no time or distance, can ever change
their love to us.   Why should we not think of them, and
speak of them here and now ?   Nothing will more endear
our Lord to us than the thought of what He was to them.
Nothing will so prompt us to self-surrender as the remembrance that into His hands they committed their spirits.
The name they confessed, shall it not be doubly dear to
us, now they are gone ?   The world is cold because the
best and warmest seem to have left it, but here in spirit
our hearts meet with them again, as, pledging anew in this
holy cup our love to Christ, we receive assurance from Him
that they are not dead but only sleeping, and that for us
He will keep against that day all that we have committed
unto Him.

    But, however it may be of others, of one, surely, it is
fitting that mention be made here to-day—of that noblest
of Christians and saintliest of men, SAMUEL GILMAN
BROWN.   So often of late has he sat beside me at this table
that I turn instinctively, as I speak his name, almost as if
expecting to behold him.   How many times within the last
few years has he broken for you this bread, or poured out
this cup.   He stood here almost as a spiritual presence, so
pure and good we knew him to be.   Before his lips opened,
we read in the gentle lines of his lovely face the peace of
God which passeth understanding, and the holy calm of a
spirit in communion with its Lord.   Then he spoke to us,
and listening we were lifted toward his own level.   Simple
words they always were, as suited the occasion,—truths to
Christian ears the most familiar, but *his* speaking them
seemed to make them new to us, and more than ever true.

The words and *the man* helped us to realize, as we could not otherwise, what we do as often as we eat this bread and drink this wine. Or if he prayed, as we followed him access to the throne of grace seemed easy, prayer real and blessed, and even while he yet pleaded the answer seemed to rest in peace and blessing upon our souls. Rare occasions these, dear friends, never to be ours again. Yet I doubt me if we could have prized them more, even had we known but four short months ago that then for the last time we bowed to receive his favorite benediction : " Now the God of peace, that brought again from the dead our Lord Jesus, that great Shepherd of the sheep, through the blood of the everlasting covenant, make you perfect in every good work to do His will, working in you that which is well pleasing in His sight, through Jesus Christ ; to whom be glory forever and ever. Amen."

Others know better than we, and can better tell, how great the loss sustained in the death of President BROWN in all the broader avenues of life in which he walked, by the cause of higher education, for instance, to which he had devoted his life, and by the Church at large, in whose progress and welfare he maintained so true an interest.

And as for what he was in his own home, and to his family, it is not for any to tell, none *can* tell. The hearts most bereaved by his death know, not their own bitterness only, but the rich treasures they have held, and still hold forever and forever. It is not for a stranger, nor even for a friend, to intermeddle therewith. There are fathers who enable us to understand what God means when He says : " Thou shalt call me, My Father." There are homes that anticipate Heaven.

But what Dr. BROWN was to us we know, and now that he is gone we delight to tell it. Not soon again shall we have to speak of such a man—a man so wise and noble—a Christian so simple and strong, pre-eminent in every relation, and yet to the plainest of his brethren a wise counsellor, a generous helper, a true and abiding

friend.   The fellowship which we, as a church, were permitted to enjoy with him was brief, to be sure, and much
interrupted by his absences from home, but his coming
among us was of itself a blessing from the Father, and his
presence here was a continual benediction.   He was always
ready to render kindly aid, and therefore often preached
from this pulpit, and, as often as he did, we were both attracted and impressed, both instructed and encouraged, by
his words.   To look into his face, it was often said among
us, to behold " the beaming light and sweetness of his
countenance," was as good as a sermon, so radiant was it
with kindly feeling.   In his sermons, as in himself, there
was always a blending, in happiest proportions, of strength
and beauty.   There were precision of language and logi-
cal sequence, with all the graces of a chaste and flowing
rhetoric.   And over all, and in all, there was an undefined
influence, purifying and elevating, breathing with spiritual
life.   In all that he regarded as fundamental to Christianity
he had unfaltering faith ; his frequent and happy expression
of that faith was to more than one mind among us, prone
to doubt, most reassuring.   He was intensely alive to all
that is new in religious thought and criticism, yet he held
with firm grasp the old that is true.   Above all, his faith
in Jesus the Christ knew no wavering ; nay, it grew ever
stronger and deeper, until now that faith is lost in sight.
Those sermons will not soon be forgotten, and, when forgotten, their influence will abide, inciting us to something
of his own benignity and saintliness.

In personal contact with Dr. BROWN, even more than
from the pulpit, was felt the singular fascination of his
beautiful character.   Truly, he was a man to draw every-
body's love.   Serene in his strength, maintaining always
the reserve of a true Christian dignity, how gentle he was,
and how affectionate.   Even if he were reviled, he reviled
not again.   Mention was once made to him, in my hearing,
of one who had done him a most manifest wrong, and, ap-
pealed to for his opinion, Dr. BROWN would only say:

" I so little understand the nature of such a man that I am sure I am not competent to judge him." Such charity of judgment he always manifested. His views on all subjects were positive and well defined, and where principle was concerned he was firm as a rock, yet such was his transparent goodness and integrity that he was as little apt to give as to take offence. Gentle in his speech, thoughtful of others, exemplary always and in all things, no wonder that we loved him so well.

We may never again have such a man among us; that we have had him, even for a little while, we will ever remember as one of God's great blessings to this church. We give him back his own words, spoken from this pulpit, of the late Dr. Samuel W. Fisher:

" The lessons of a noble and faithful life, whose last years were spent among us, are patent to us all; excellences which we see we may try to imitate, defects to avoid, but even to recognize and acknowledge the truly good and great is itself a step toward the good.

" Happy for us, if we each, as the shadows lengthen, are filled with the hope which sustained him, and, as the evening draws on, can as serenely give up our account for the day's work, feeling that it has been faithfully done."

VIII.

OTHER MEMORIAL PAPERS AND RESOLUTIONS.

MEMORIAL OF THE FACULTY OF HAMILTON COLLEGE.

ADOPTED NOVEMBER 4, 1885.

———

AT a special meeting of the Faculty of Hamilton College, held in the Library, November 4, 1885, President Darling announced the death of his predecessor in office, and the following resolutions were adopted :

Resolved, That in the death of Rev. SAMUEL GILMAN BROWN we mourn the sudden departure of an accomplished educator, author, and preacher, who for fifteen years adorned the highest office of Hamilton College with the highest gifts of scholarship, wisdom, and personal worth, and who in all the duties and amenities of life, as an executive officer, as teacher, companion, and friend, was always true to the noblest standard of Christian character.

Resolved, That we tender to the afflicted family and friends of our departed ex-President the assurances of our heartfelt sympathy with them in their irreparable bereavement, and that we invoke for them the consolations that can only come from the Supreme Comforter.

Resolved, That it would be in keeping with our wishes and our estimate of what is most befitting, that the grave of our venerable ex-President should be made in our College Cemetery, where it would be surrounded with memorials of the crowning labors of his most useful and honorable life, and where it would help to perpetuate the good influences of his exalted character.

Resolved, That we, as a Faculty, attend the funeral service of ex-President BROWN, and that our College exercises be suspended on the day of this service.

Resolved, That these resolutions be entered on the minutes of the Faculty, that they be presented to the family of ex-President BROWN, that they be read in the College Chapel, and that they be published.

MEMORIAL OF THE FACULTY OF DARTMOUTH COLLEGE.

The Faculty of Dartmouth College desire to place on record their high appreciation of the life and character of the late SAMUEL GILMAN BROWN, D.D., LL.D., and of the excellent services rendered by him to the cause of good literature and sound Christian education. They gratefully recognize his long and useful connection with this College, and his influence upon its culture and its reputation; and they will ever hold him in affectionate remembrance as an accomplished scholar and writer, a diligent instructor, a wise counsellor, a genial companion, and a Christian gentleman, who closed a most honorable career at a ripe age and widely lamented.

They would also tender their cordial sympathy to his afflicted family, and rejoice with them in the abundant consolations that are connected with the history of such a life.

MEMORIAL OF THE FACULTY OF BOWDOIN COLLEGE.

ADOPTED NOVEMBER 4, 1885.

Died at Utica, N. Y., November 4, 1885, Rev. SAMUEL GILMAN BROWN, D.D., LL.D., Professor of Mental and Moral Philosophy in Bowdoin College, 1883–85.

At a meeting of the Academical Faculty of Bowdoin College, November 4th, the following Memorial was adopted to be incorporated with the records of the Faculty, and to be communicated to the family of the deceased.

The sad intelligence of the death of our former colleague, and our beloved friend, Rev. Dr. BROWN, brings to us a keen sense of personal bereavement to which we cannot forbear to give utterance, while it permits us also to unite in an expression of profound respect for his character, and of affectionate veneration for his memory.

The years during which he was associated with us in the service of the College were so filled with the evidences of his gracious and kindly spirit; his intercourse with us, and with all whom he met, had in it such a charm of courtesy and of Christian culture, that he bound us all to himself by ties of no common regard.

It gives us pleasure, even while we mourn his death, to remember and to bear grateful witness to the unselfish devotion and ability with which he served the interests of the College and the pupils who enjoyed his instruction; the cheerfulness with which he undertook, and the success with which he performed, the special services that were asked of him from time to time; the enthusiasm with which he entered into all plans that were formed to promote the welfare of the College, and labored to make them effective; and the generosity with which he strove, in all ways, to enlarge the influence and maintain the honor and the Christian character of the College.

We desire to offer to the family of this departed servant of God, who has been permitted to fill his life with so much of useful and distinguished service, the assurances of our respectful and sincere sympathy in their bereavement, while we give thanks, with them, for a life which has been so rich in the fruits of a consecrated discipleship.

MEMORIAL OF CHI ALPHA.*

PRESENTED BY THE REV. ROSWELL D. HITCHCOCK, D.D., LL.D., PRESIDENT OF THE UNION THEOLOGICAL SEMINARY, AND ADOPTED BY CHI ALPHA NOVEMBER 21, 1885.

IN MEMORIAM.

SAMUEL GILMAN BROWN, D.D., LL.D., was born in North Yarmouth, Me., January 4, 1813, and died in Utica, N. Y., November 4, 1885.

His father was Francis Brown, President of Dartmouth College from 1815 to 1820. The son graduated at Dartmouth in 1831, and at Andover Theological Seminary in 1837. From 1838 to 1840 he travelled and studied in Europe. For twenty-seven years he was Professor in Dartmouth College,—first of Oratory, from 1840 to 1863, and then of Mental Philosophy, from 1863 to 1867. From 1867 to 1881 he was President of Hamilton College. In the last two years of his life he

---

* An association of ministers in New York City.

had charge of the Senior Class in Bowdoin College, in whose neighbor-hood the first two years of his life were spent.

In all these positions he earned for himself an enviable reputation. He was an accurate scholar, and an admirable teacher; of catholic judgment, unerring taste, fine, gracious manners, and lofty Christian purpose.

Chi Alpha remembers him with lively interest and affection. For the last eighteen years of his life he was frequently our guest. On October 17, 1885, less than three weeks before he died, we showed our esteem for him by a vote of permanent hospitality. Our sense of personal bereavement could hardly be keener, had his name been standing on our Roll of Members.

To his son, our brother, Professor Francis Brown, to his widow, and to all the surviving children and grandchildren, we tender the assurance of our sincerest sympathy.

MEMORIAL OF THE ONEIDA HISTORICAL SOCIETY.

OFFERED BY GENERAL CHARLES W. DARLING, AND

ADOPTED NOVEMBER 30, 1885.

Whereas, It has pleased Almighty God, in His all-wise and mysterious providence, to remove from the sphere of his earthly labors to his eternal rest His faithful servant, Rev. SAMUEL G. BROWN, D.D.,

Resolved, That in the death of Rev. Dr. BROWN this society has lost a faithful, earnest member, endowed with many noble and Christian virtues.

Resolved, That to the bereaved family we tender our heartfelt sympathy, with the assurance that he whom they mourn will ever be held in remembrance by us; and we request that the officers of this meeting communicate to them that expression of our sympathy, with a copy of this preamble and resolution.

MEMORIAL OF THE PRESBYTERY OF UTICA.

ADOPTED APRIL 14, 1886.

Whereas, The death of Rev. SAMUEL G. BROWN, D.D., LL.D., has occurred since our last regular meeting, therefore

Resolved, That we put on record our sense of personal and public loss in his death. Coming into our body on being called to the Presidency of Hamilton College, he won our admiration and respect as a superior educator, and a gentleman of rare culture and refinement. Though seldom prominent in the councils of the Presbytery, we sadly miss his genial presence and the sweet influence of his high-toned Christian character.

MEMORIAL OF "THE CLUB," UTICA, N. Y.

" The Club," of Utica, N. Y., an association of gentlemen for literary purposes, of which Dr. BROWN was an active member, has printed since his death a paper on the history of the Club, prepared by him and read in 1879. To this paper, as printed, is prefixed an artotype portrait—from the same negative with that used for this Memorial—and a commemorative note, from which the following is an extract ; it is understood that the writer is the Hon. Ellis H. Roberts, LL.D.:

" His wide range of reading and meditation, his acquaintance with the themes which occupy men's minds and concern institutions and government, his familiarity with distinguished persons in many fields of labor, and his intimate conversance with the best authors in prose and poetry, in our own and other tongues, illustrated the ripeness of culture, the activity and scope of intellectual life, the fulness of manhood which we all recognize. .

" His mastery of the English language was as apparent in the informal talks of our little circle as in his most elaborate productions, and it was the simple beauty and richness of beaten gold at hand for daily use. His social and moral qualities were such as few attain. They were the expression of a soul unselfish, aspiring, true, and worthy, taking thankfully the good in his fellows, generous but not blind to their faults, attuned to the perpetual melody of principle and thought and life.

" ' Such harmony is in immortal souls.' "

MEMORIAL OF THE DARTMOUTH ALUMNI ASSOCIATION OF THE NORTHWEST.

ADOPTED AT THE FIFTH ANNUAL REUNION, JANUARY 15, 1886.

Whereas, Recently, three of the most eminent members* of the Faculty of Dartmouth College during the last half century have departed this life,

---

* See Appendix VIII.

Resolved, That we desire to express our appreciation of the value of their long and faithful service in their respective departments ; and as many of us were under their instruction, we gladly put on record our testimony to their ability and success as teachers ; and we desire also to express the hope that our Alma Mater may ever have in her corps of instructors men of the accomplished scholarship and refinement of Professor BROWN, the fidelity and gentle spirit of Professor NOYES, the full knowledge and "large roundabout common-sense" of Professor SANBORN.

———

Attention was called to the death of the three ex-Professors at other meetings of Dartmouth Alumni, during the winter of 1885–86, *e.g.,* in Boston, New York, Washington, and Cincinnati, and honors were paid to their memory. Special mention may be made of the meeting in Boston, January 27, 1886, the remarks there of the Hon. Walbridge A. Field, and the warm tribute of the Hon. John L. Hayes to the character of Dr. BROWN, his college classmate and life-long friend.

———

The Faculty of Dartmouth College has requested the Rev. WILLIAM J. TUCKER, D.D., Professor in Andover Theological Seminary, a graduate of Dartmouth in 1861, and now a member of its Board of Trustees, to deliver in Hanover an address commemorative of Drs. BROWN, NOYES, and SANBORN.

IX.

[A few contributions to this Memorial from friends who saw much of Dr. Brown during the later years of his life are here grouped together.]

From Professor Edward North, L.H.D., of Hamilton College.

———

The leading events in President Brown's administration, briefly stated in their historical order, were these :

1. The erection in 1867 of the new President's house, to replace the house built for President Backus in 1813.

2. The election in 1868 of Professor E. W. Root to the Childs Professorship of Chemistry, and the election of Professor A. H. Chester to the same chair, after the death of Professor Root in 1870.

3. The interior renovation of the College Chapel in 1868, and the introduction of the Chapel organ in 1870.

4. The election in 1869 of Rev. A. G. Hopkins to the Latin Professorship, as the successor of Professor W. N. McHarg.

5. The first New York Reunion of Hamilton Alumni, held at the Astor House, January 21, 1869, with addresses by the Hon. Charles P. Kirkland, President Brown, Chancellor Pruyn, Daniel Huntington, Professor T. W. Dwight, and others.

6. The election in 1870 of Professor Samuel D. Wilcox to the Kingsley Chair of Rhetoric and Elocution, as the successor of Professor Anson J. Upson ; and the election in 1872 of Professor Henry A. Frink as the successor of Professor Wilcox.

7. The election in 1870 of Professor Chester Huntington to the Chair of Physics, after he had served the College one year as a tutor.

8. The election in 1871 of Rev. Dr. John W. Mears to the Albert Barnes Professorship of Moral Philosophy.

9. The inauguration in 1872 of the Perry H. Smith Library Hall and Art Gallery, with addresses by President Brown, Rev. Dr. N.

W. Goertner, Hon. O. S. Williams, Rev. Dr. Henry Kendall, Rev. Dr. James Eells, and others.

10. The dedication in 1873 of the monument in the College Cemetery to Rev. Samuel Kirkland, with addresses by President BROWN, Hon. O. S. Williams, Hon. Horatio Seymour, Dr. S. B. Woolworth, Daniel Sconondoa, and others.

11. The restoration and reopening of South College in 1874, under its new name of Hungerford Hall, in honor of Hon. John N. Hungerford, of Elmira.

12. The public services commemorative of Rev. Dr. S. W. Fisher (who died January 18, 1874), with addresses by Judge W. J. Bacon, President BROWN, and Rev. Dr. Thomas J. Brown.

13. The appointment in 1874 of Professor H. C. G. Brandt as Instructor in Modern Languages.

14. The amendment of the College Charter, in 1875, giving to the graduates of the College the privilege of electing four representatives in the Board of Trustees.

15. The Utica reception of Dr. C. H. F. Peters, in June, 1875, after his return from New Zealand, with addresses by Judge W. J. Bacon, Judge Johnson, Dr. John P. Gray, and others.

16. The placing in the Chapel belfry, June 4, 1877, of the Howard Clock, presented to the College by Mr. John Wanamaker, of Philadelphia, Pa.

17. The election in 1878 of Professor Ambrose P. Kelsey to the Chair of Natural History, endowed by Mrs. Valeria G. Stone, of Malden, Mass.

18. The election in 1880 of Professor Oren Root, Jr., to the Professorship of Mathematics, as the successor of Professor Oren Root, Sr.

That the administration of Dr. BROWN was fruitful of good results is clearly inferable from the foregoing statement of facts. His record may be looked at in another way by comparing it with the record of his predecessors in the same office. Dr. Azel Backus held the Presidency three years, and gave 33 diplomas to graduates and honorary alumni. Dr. Henry Davis gave 329 diplomas in seventeen classes; Dr. Sereno E. Dwight gave 39 diplomas in two classes; Dr. Joseph Penny 53 diplomas in three classes; Dr. Simeon North 661 diplomas in nineteen classes; Dr. Samuel W. Fisher 306 diplomas in eight classes; Dr. SAMUEL G. BROWN 775 diplomas in fifteen classes.

Memories of the daily life of Dr. BROWN bring unfailing satisfaction to one who walked with him, talked with him, and worked with him, on College Hill, for fourteen busy, anxious years. To meet him as he started for the morning chapel was finding new sources of enjoyment and new strength for the duties of the day. His sensitive nature was quickly responsive to the inspirations of a new day in early summer, to the subtle fragrances from the trees and the lawns, to the changing colors of the distant hills, and the songs of birds. His manner of conducting a religious service was very impressive in its simplicity, its reverent earnestness, and the entire absence of anything like personal display. His sermons were wholesome food for thought, solid material for the building of a noble character, generous helps to young men who were striving to be made beautiful within. His wide reading brought to him for argument or illustration all the treasures of the past, and, in the use of history and literature, his trained intellect, his ripe wisdom, his rhetorical skill were unerring guides. A volume of his sermons and addresses would be a valuable addition to our national literature.

At meetings of the College Faculty, where character sometimes meets its crucial test, President BROWN never lost his self-control, or his habitual courtesy and love of even-handed justice. His hatred of all crooked self-seeking was intense. In dealing with selfish intrigues and shams it was possible for him to "be angry and sin not," when his own daily life and conversation were so exemplary in all that is pure, unselfish, honorable, and of good report. To say these things is only repeating what has been already said in more befitting words in the addresses that followed the sudden death of Dr. BROWN. His life and character will bear the light of close analysis and scrutiny. He will be enrolled on the list of prominent Americans as one whose profound and accurate learning was a power used without pedantry or ostentation, whose intellectual strength was a sword wreathed with myrtle, whose home-life was as beautiful and sweet as his public career was honorably useful and blameless.

————

FROM THE REV. ISAAC S. HARTLEY, D.D., OF UTICA, N. Y.

No words at my command can adequately express the loss I have sustained in the sudden death of your loved and honored father. While I had known him many years, and occasionally visited him at his home, it was not till he became a fellow-townsman that my acquaintance grew into friendship, and that that friendship bloomed and ripened into love (may I say?) as pure and unsullied as bud that ever unfolded.

During the last few years, when he was comparatively free from active duties and at home, he honored me almost daily with his companionship; and as in many respects we had common interests and common pleasures, these many hours will long be remembered. . . . His simplicity and gracefulness of manner, his ease, sincerity, and naturalness were exceedingly winsome, and led you at once to feel that you were in the society of one to whom you could tell, if need be, your most hidden secrets, and experience no check, nor suffer betrayal. Few sooner gained your confidence or were more easily approached; fewer still more sympathetic and listening. His extensive and varied reading, his close and exhaustive study, his knowledge of philosophy and familiarity with the teachings of the schools, made him quick and ready in thought; while his scholarly taste, united with a faultless style, brought that thought to you clothed in the richest yet simplest apparel. I believe few could more easily command their attainments, or have them respond more promptly to appeal. When, as frequently happened, questions relating to the State came up for remark, the readiness with which he discussed them and his reference to errors made by other nationalities in solving like or similar difficulties were truly phenomenal. . . . Themes social, economic, and philanthropic found in him also a devout student; and whenever alluded to he discussed them with unusual fluency, his words ever revealing previous reflection, as well as the possession of the calm, judicial mind. . . .

But the subject to which, perhaps, he most frequently reverted in these hours by the way, as well as when surrounded with his more intimate friends, was Christianity and its influence; what it had wrought, what it was working, and what he believed it would some day include in its holy grasp. With him it was no mere creed or set of defined doctrines, but a life, a force—and a divine life and force. . . . No one could spend an hour with your father without admiring his catholicity of spirit. . . . In the ministerial meeting his presence was anxiously looked for, and when he spoke on the question under discussion, his wisdom, humility, and sweetness of spirit wooed and won. . . . While most judicious in commending, he was very courteous in reproof. His courteousness was not artfulness, any more than his honesty and integrity were guarded. I never knew him speak a harsh word. He seldom talked about the living, there seemingly being a sacredness about personality which he was unwilling to disturb. Nor did he carry any concealed armor. . . . I pray that the spirit of his life may not be lost upon me. Sometimes I find myself

> . . . " Waiting for a hand,
> A hand that can be clasp'd no more."

4

As he looks down upon me from my study wall, I feel I am the constant recipient of a silent benediction. In our common loneliness and sorrow, how comforting, however, to know that

> " The dead are like the stars by day,
>   Unseen by mortal eye,
>   But not extinct ; they hold their way
>   In glory through the sky."

FROM THE REV. WILLIAM P. FISHER, PASTOR OF THE CONGRE-
GATIONAL CHURCH, BRUNSWICK, ME.

In the two years of Dr. BROWN'S teaching in Bowdoin College, the esteem and appreciation were generally accorded to him which were naturally his due. . . . But I accounted myself especially fortu-nate in the circumstances which allowed me his intimacy. The varied, entertaining, and instructive conversation, the inexhaustible familiarity with men and things, the unfailing courtesy and uniform cheerfulness, the prudent counsels, the hearty sympathy and aid in emergencies, were greatly valued at the time as they are held in grateful remem-brance. That benevolent face, handsome with its fresh color and white locks, remains to me the representative of a graceful, gracious, and devout old age. It was a rare friendship. I used sometimes to ask myself what must be the value and delight of such a companion-ship in all the life. It was delightful to see the exceptional charm of his good-fellowship in society, continued in the intimacy of the home circle, and only improving with intimacy.

In connection with a memorial window in the Congregational Church at Brunswick, Me., commemorating the Rev. Professor Alpheus Spring Packard, D.D., of Bowdoin College,* the Rev. W. P. Fisher made, on Sunday, November 15, 1885, a few remarks about Dr. BROWN, to which the following extract refers :

---

* Alpheus Spring Packard, D.D., was born at Chelmsford, Mass., December 23, 1798 ; graduated at Bowdoin College in 1816 ; tutor there from 1819 to 1824 ; Professor of the Greek and Latin Languages from 1824 to 1865 ; and Collins Pro-fessor of Natural and Revealed Religion from 1865 until his death. He was or-dained to the Congregational Ministry May 16, 1850, and received the degree of Doctor of Divinity from Bowdoin College in 1869. He died suddenly at Squirrel Island, Me., July 13, 1884, having made the excursion from Brunswick in the com-pany of a few friends, of whom Dr. BROWN was one.

[*Brunswick Telegraph*, November 20, 1885.]

The choice of the style of window was greatly due to the efforts of the late Rev. Dr. BROWN, whose knowledge of men across the water and the architectural designs of foreign windows aided very much to secure the tasteful and appropriate memorial which has been placed in the north transept gallery of the Congregational Church, of which Professor Packard was so long a member and officer. The tender and appreciative tribute paid to the memory of Rev. Dr. BROWN by the pastor was listened to with deep interest by all his hearers. The two venerated officers of the College were in intimate association during the two years of Dr. BROWN'S residence among us, and were together when the final hour came for the beloved Professor Packard. They were alike in their Christian courtesy, their literary tastes, and both, while deeply religious men, were genial and social to a remarkable degree, and interested in the welfare of all around them. The window may therefore be considered a memorial to both.

X.

FROM THE UTICA MORNING HERALD.

NOVEMBER 5, 1885.

THOSE who knew Dr. BROWN well could not fail to be charmed by the graces of his character and the generous and catholic spirit which pervaded all his acts. His Christian charity under trial was a model for imitation. It was the fruit of inwrought conviction and principle, as well as of a disposition naturally attractive. His scholarship was very thorough and without a particle of affectation. He was deeply versed in English literature of every period, and was a master of the works of the great orators who have made glorious our mother tongue. In command of the English language he had very few peers, and his mastery was manifest on the least formal occasion.

Dr. BROWN mingled with men and attracted them to him. His acquaintance was large with the most noted and the most accomplished of our scholars and statesmen, as well as with clergymen of all denominations. He enjoyed the society of well-informed persons, and always had something to communicate calculated to arouse thought. His companionship was delightful, and without any assumption he was recognized in every gathering as a leader of men. With the modesty of scholarship, he had the strength of a full and true character, of opinions well founded, of accomplishments which were the fruitage of a life of study and of work.

As President of Hamilton College, Dr. BROWN accomplished results which will be remembered as long as the institution endures. He won the affection as he commanded the esteem of all of his pupils. His teaching was without the least attempt at sensation. It was earnest, genuine, and suggestive, and fruitful. No student ever gave heed to his instruction without permanent effect upon his training and culture. Since his resignation as president he has retained his position as trustee and as a member of the Executive Committee, and has rendered valuable service to the institution. His loss will be felt in its councils. As an educator he held to the conservative methods, to thoroughness of discipline, and to study for its own sake and for the enlightenment and elevation of character. Such a man is a torch-bearer wherever his steps lead.

FROM THE UTICA OBSERVER.

November 4, 1885.

So symmetrical a character as Dr. BROWN'S is not easily analysed. In all directions so evenly developed was he, that it is difficult to point to this quality or that as the secret of his greatness. There was in him the rarest combination of strength and gentleness. No man was firmer in his convictions or truer to the Christian principles by which, throughout all his life, he had sought to guide both thought and action. At the same time none was ever more tolerant and charitable, both because a tender, loving, sympathetic heart controlled and directed his strength, and because his large knowledge as a student of history, of humanity and human affairs, delivered him from partisanship, and made him incapable of the egotism which manifests itself in zeal against all opinions and practices which are not its own. He was pre-eminently a scholar, broad and liberal, bringing to every subject a sincere and earnest mind, capable by nature and through long training of calm, independent, and thorough investigation. His enthusiasm was most kindled by his life-long labors as an instructor, to which work he brought inspiration joined with unlimited painstaking. Everywhere he was recognized as one of the foremost teachers of our country. He was, too, a most graceful writer and speaker, and some of the best work of his life was done in the pulpit, where the strength of his mind and the goodness of his heart were equally manifested.

FROM THE UTICA DAILY PRESS.

November 5, 1885.

Dr. BROWN was a man of many amiable qualities and rare ability. As a scholar he had few equals, and he was a man of remarkable literary culture. He was a strong and clear writer, and his articles were always both entertaining and instructive. He was best known in this vicinity as President of Hamilton College. In his administration of the affairs of that institution, his work was characterized by honesty

of purpose and faithful discharge of every duty. Of a gentle manner and a kindly heart, he won the respect of all who knew him. He
was a man of firm. conviction and unswerving devotion to what he
regarded as right. Wherever he spoke, and whatever the occasion,
Hamilton had an able representative. In his intercourse with the
students he was friendly, and bore himself in such a way as to impress
them in his favor. As a disciplinarian he had the courage to do
whatever he thought the case required, but preferred mild measures
where they would accomplish the desired result. His sermons were
always full of thought and power, and were listened to attentively.
His services as a preacher were much sought, and he spoke to large
audiences when he could do so consistently with his duties at the college. It was, however, in the class-room that Dr. BROWN was most
at home. He was as familiar with his subjects as with the merest
rudiments of science, and had invaluable resources of mind and in-
formation. He taught all the text-book suggested and more, and
added observations and ideas of his own that were of priceless
worth. His kindly way endeared him to the students and gained their
affections. His lectures to the classes showed his wonderful scholas-
tic attainments, and never failed to win the admiration of his hearers.
No one was ever absent from his place when Dr. BROWN was to
lecture. His relations with the Faculty were such as to gain for him
their hearty support. In his family he was an affectionate husband
and father, and his home life was always pleasant. To know Dr.
BROWN was to admire his ability, to be charmed by his manner, and
to respect his Christian manliness.

FROM THE HANOVER (N. H.) GAZETTE.

NOVEMBER 7, 1885.

The death of Rev. Dr. SAMUEL GILMAN BROWN, announced by
telegraph Wednesday, brings sadness to the hearts of the old friends
and neighbors in Hanover, to whom he was so well known, and by
whom he was so greatly beloved. This is not the time and place for
an extended eulogy, but it seems fitting to say a few words here and
now of one whose life among us for many years was so helpful, so
courteous, and so kind ; whose departure has been so permanently
regretted, whose work in the College has left such enduring influence,
and whose sudden death, at Utica, N. Y., will be so deeply deplored.

    .   .   .   .

It was greatly desired and hoped that after his work there [at Hamilton College] was finished, and he could turn to less wearing and per-

plexing duties, we might have him back again in the old familiar home, and among the friends of his early life.   It will always be a source of regret to those who loved him here that this hope was frustrated. But it has been very pleasant for us to know how fully his heart was here, and to receive the cordial clasp of his hand in his not infrequent visits to Hanover.   In Dr. BROWN'S death the last link seems to be severed which bound us to those early days of the College, when his father's young hand had the helm amid the troubled sea of a conflict which came near destroying its very life.   One by one we are going to join the peaceful sleepers in the old graveyard.   But our work does not go there with us.   Force is never lost.   We are glad to know that every blow struck for the right will vibrate on forever, and every example of a pure and noble life will continue to do good somehow and somewhere throughout the coming ages.   The words of Dr. Gurley's hymn express the aspirations of our hearts :

'' Kept peaceful in the midst of strife,
    Forgiving and forgiven ;
 So may we walk the pilgrim life,
    And find the path to heaven.''

FROM THE NEW YORK EVANGELIST.

NOVEMBER 12, 1885.

The sudden death of ex-President BROWN, of Hamilton College, has carried unusual keenness of grief to a very large circle of devoted and admiring friends.   His rare antecedents and opportunities, his noble qualities of head and heart, his broad and varied culture, his fine Christian character, and his long, distinguished service in conspicuous positions, are now all gathered to a focus in our recollection of the man and his work.   Such completeness and symmetry, both of character and career, are seldom achieved. . . .   His pupils always spoke of him with great affection, reverence, and gratitude.

The last few weeks of his busy life were passed in New York City with his son, Francis Brown, Professor in the Union Theological Seminary [and other friends].   On Friday, October 30th, he was present in Adams Chapel to hear Archdeacon Farrar, and offered the introductory prayer.   Saturday evening, October 31st, he attended the regular weekly meeting of Chi Alpha, a clerical association, of which he had been made a permanent guest.   The Monday following he rejoined his family at Utica.   On Tuesday he complained of pectoral oppression, indicative of heart disease, and early on Wednesday morning, the 4th of November, died instantaneously, without a struggle, and apparently without pain. There was no movement of hand or feature. The heart simply stood still, and the face looked calm and sweet in its last repose.

On Friday morning, November 6th, a funeral service was held in the Westminster Presbyterian Church, Utica (which President BROWN had attended), conducted by the pastor, Dr. Thomas J. Brown, assisted by Dr. Isaac S. Hartley, of the Reformed Church, Utica; Dr. Thomas B. Hudson, of Clinton; and Professor A. Grosvenor Hopkins, of Hamilton College. The latter made a somewhat extended address, which was singularly appropriate, touching, and impressive.

The body of the dead President was borne on Saturday to his old home, in Hanover, N. H., where his parents and two of his children lie buried. The interment was on Sunday afternoon, the 8th of November.

FROM THE INDEPENDENT.

NEW YORK, NOVEMBER 12, 1885.

From his father Dr. BROWN inherited many of his characteristics, and, to a singular degree, his career. From him was derived his refined elegance of person and manner, his academic type and scholarly tastes, his love of philosophy and of music, and the faultless style and diction which were the delight of his friends.

.   .   .   .

Like his father, he was invited to the Presidency of Hamilton, though, unlike him, he was persuaded to accept the office. He was a finished and thoughtful preacher, a useful teacher, a fine scholar, and a man of the highest refinement, purity, simplicity, and fidelity. As professor and as president he sustained himself with dignity and wisdom, which shone the brightest in adverse circumstances. The administrative power, as a ruler of men and manager of affairs, which enabled the father to carry Dartmouth triumphantly through its contest against President Wheelock and the State of New Hampshire, and which won the admiration of Webster, Jeremiah Mason, and Rufus Choate, took, in the son, a different direction, and appeared in the fine qualities of his mind and heart.

FROM THE ABBOT COURANT.

ANDOVER, MASS., JUNE, 1886.

It may be said of Dr. BROWN that, as his spirit and speech were under strong self-control, so were his mental powers held under the same masterful command. In his home, always made sunny by his presence, "the study" was the favorite family resort. Wife and children and other members of the household, with guests not a few—who so often and so cordially were counted among them—were always welcomed there, and however he might be absorbed in writing or reading, his heart was always so "at leisure from itself" that book or pen could at once be laid aside, to give undivided attention to whatever called for his sympathy or interest from the oldest to the youngest of his large family. No interruption could break the calm flow of his thoughts. The pen would be again taken up, and the thread of thought run on as if the silence had been unbroken and no jar felt. It was an extraordinary exception, and only when writing under great pressure of time, that he would ask to be alone. His fondness for music was so great that, so far from being annoyed at the sound of the piano when writing a sermon or a lecture, it was to him an unconscious inspiration, and he would say, "I write the better for it."

The higher forms of music were to him a great delight. He often said that whatever of correct taste he had in this direction was largely due to his familiarity when in college with the old Handel and Haydn collection of church music.

The symphonies of Mendelssohn and Beethoven—his favorite Oratorios of "The Messiah," "The Creation," and "Elijah"—the Masses of Haydn and Mozart, yielded rich satisfaction to a soul so attuned to all that is high and grand and sacred in art no less than in letters. This keen sensitiveness to the beautiful, the delicate, the noble, wherever found, which gave such freshness and intensity to his enjoyment of life, never lost its fine edge.

XI.

[Many letters of sympathy have been received from all parts of the country and from other lands. A few extracts are here given, the first being from a recent graduate of Hamilton College :]

.　　.　　.　　.　　.　　.　　.　　.　　.

THREE men stand out as great factors in my life : Dr. N——, Dr. BROWN, and my father. I cannot be too thankful that before entering college I had the advantage of the high estimate which Dr. N—— and my father had of Dr. BROWN, and so was prepared to give him my confidence. I think that it was during the summer of the year in which I wént to Clinton that he occupied Dr. N——'s pulpit. I remember very well the pleasure which his sermons gave my father. . . . Then followed the four years at Hamilton, during which I learned to love as well as to admire Dr. BROWN.

The afternoon on which I received the news of his death I read to myself, and then to a friend, the address which he delivered in memory of his predecessor, Dr. Fisher, and went to the Public Library for his " Life of Choate," but it was out. I came back to my room and sat down, thinking I would send some expression to the *Evangelist*, for it seemed as though a tribute should appear from some one of the many students who were under him ; but I found that I could not carry out this wish. If I had loved him less, if he had been more angular, I might have written something ; but he stood before me in such completeness as a Christian scholar that I was afraid to touch his memory.

Some men put much of themselves into favorite phrases. How often Dr. BROWN used to say in eulogy upon some man of letters, like G. P. Marsh, that " he was a lover of learning." Surely he himself was that ; and in such an unpretentious way, after the manner of Socrates, who preferred the title of "a lover of wisdom " to that of "a wise man," he would, perhaps, have described himself upon his intellectual side. Into his estimate of himself in this and in other directions there entered a fine Christian humility, which added its charm to those rare intellectual qualities and qualifications, into the possession of which he had come by inheritance and training.

I am thankful to be able to retain the memory of a college president who was not disproportionately developed so as to invite an unfortunate imitation of special points, but who set before me the model of a complete Christian education. He was instinctively and by culture a gentleman. How large in conception and faultless in execution was all his literary work! How varied and profound his attainments! Indeed, he was a true lover of all learning. More than all this, he was in possession of a Christian character, which trial only served to refine and make visible to others. "It has not been my fortune," said Senator Hawley at our Alumni dinner, "to come in contact with a sweeter Christian spirit."

We are inclined to feel in such a death that too much is buried; but we ought rather to be thankful that the best is imperishable, that "life in death survives, and the uninterrupted breath inspires" many and many a life.

[Other friends sent the following :]

How loyally, how royally, he loved his friends! With what a brave and cheery spirit he met the trials of every day—with what patience and forbearance he met wrong-doing—with what courage and persistency he battled for the right! It seems fitting that he should have been spared long suffering, and the decay of mental power, and the anguish of parting from those he loved so fondly—and that the one little moment should have placed his feet on the *other side.*

He who always was so full of bright, loving, gracious life—it hardly seems possible to associate death with him—I would rather think of the life immortal with Christ which he has entered, where there is no more death, nor sorrow, nor pain, and where all tears are wiped away.

How beautiful it is to go out of life so peacefully! It seemed so in keeping with the repose which President BROWN always carried in his presence to almost without pain pass out of life into the unknown blessedness of the heavenly life—so like his Master here, to be made perfect "even as He is perfect" there. Aside from the loss to the dear ones, how great is that to the world when such a great, true heart and noble intellect is taken from it! But I like to think that the power of such lives in the world does not end at death, but that God may use them and permit them to finish their work in His own way.

———

After such a noble, honored, and useful life, translation seems rather the saint's reward than a calamity to be prayed against, and the petition of the Litany seems needed most for the friends bereft.

I congratulate you on the blessed memories and the full assurance of hope that your dear father has left to you.

———

I believe I may say with the most perfect honesty, that of all faces which ever brightened my little private office, there never was any which I was more glad to see, or which brought more geniality, brightness, and purity with it, than that of your honored father. I never enjoyed the pleasure of intimacy with him, but he so impressed me with the sweetness and worth of his humanity, the genuineness of his character as a scholar, and the refinement of his whole nature, that I always felt his presence as a benediction.

———

. . . I do not see how we can be otherwise than glad for those who have been spared the long agony of dying, and the long wear of pain—who fall at their posts, in the ripeness and fulness of their powers.

I never knew your father,—but he made the same impression upon me that he seems to have made upon all who met him, even in the slightest intercourse—the impression of a calm, sweet, and wholly harmonious nature, with the large wisdom that comes from a deep knowledge of books and life and men. The charm of his written and spoken word was felt to spring from a perfectly well-rounded and gracious personality, as well as from his full mind and varied knowledge. I think such men strengthen our belief greatly in the possibilities of humanity, and through their completeness give more than a hint and suggestion of the perfect development of the life beyond life.

XII.

[One of the letters written by Dr. Brown after his return to Utica, November 2d, was addressed to the Rev. Frederick A. Adams, Ph.D., of Brick Church, N. J., who was an old friend of College and Seminary days. It is fitting that Dr. Adams' letter addressed to one of Dr. Brown's children, under date of November 5, 1885, should close this series of extracts :]

I was startled this morning on seeing in *The Tribune* the announcement of the death of Rev. Samuel Gilman Brown, D.D., LL.D., the more because it is but a few days since your father visited me in my house, kindly taking the pains to come from New York City for that purpose. It was very pleasant, cheering, and precious. . . . S. G. Brown and I had been friends from an early time in my college life, drawn together partly by our common interest in the Handel Society. . . . I was witness of his growing power, and his harmonizing influence in the College and afterward in the Seminary. It is pleasant now to remember how, when under some unfair pressure, he had it in him to waive his own clear rights for the sake of the harmony of others. Standing where I now do, it would be right and pious to forget what it would be painful to remember. But in S. G. Brown I know of nothing that it would be painful to remember.

P. M.—I had written thus far this morning, when I was called away to the city; and on my return I found awaiting me the inclosed letter in your father's own hand. It would have been a pleasant surprise in any case to receive a letter so soon after his visit; what memories does it now awaken—now that the hand that wrote it is still! Happily was his own prayer fulfilled—he was not called to witness the decay of his own powers!

This letter, it occurs to me, may possibly be among the last that your father wrote. With this thought in mind I will make a copy of it for my own use, and send the original to you, which you may keep if you desire.

The lovely November day is drawing to its close. As I watch its fading light and think of my departed friend the lines of Herbert's little hymn come to me :

   " Sweet day, so cool, so calm, so bright ! "

In the faith expressed in its closing stanza I offer to you my word of sympathy and word of cheer.

[The letter inclosed by Dr. Adams was as follows :]

UTICA, 372 Genesee Street, November 2, 1885.

REV. FREDERICK A. ADAMS, PH.D.,

MY DEAR DOCTOR : I have no doubt that you have more knowledge of Greek in your little finger than I have in my head, and just as little doubt that your book * has given me a new impression, a new conviction, of the extreme delicacy and flexibility of the Greek language, and of the wonderful precision and capability of the Greek mind. If half what you say is true, and I dare say it is *all* true, no nation seems to be even second to the Greeks in the art of expression, and that really means in the power and facility of thought. You have compressed a marvellous amount into a very little space ; a *multum in parvo*, indeed, is your valuable little book, only I ought to find a Greek phrase to express it. I have only read a part of it, and I left it, for a time, with my son, who was looking it over with great interest. It is too good a book to make you rich ; if now, it were only a spelling-book !—but you will have your reward.

It gave me great pleasure, very great, to see you in Orange. Old friends are growing fewer every year, and I wonder that I myself am verging toward my seventy-third year, and yet with my feelings of youth and enthusiasm not much changed, certainly not extinguished. I pray that I may not lose them till I part from all ; I pray that I may have strength and the will to work as long as the day lasts ; I pray that I may never lose the sense of the divine presence and help to the very end. . . .

Very affectionately, my dear old friend, I remain,

Yours as ever,   S. G. BROWN.

---

* The Greek Prepositions.

APPENDIX.

I.

<small>THE</small> following books and pamphlets by Dr. <small>BROWN</small> have been published :

1. The Studies of an Orator; Inaugural at Dartmouth, 1840. (See below, *b.*)

2. Biography of Self-Taught Men, 1847.

3. The Spirit of a Scholar; Address before the Phi Beta Kappa Society at Dartmouth, 1847. (See below, *d.*)

4. Eulogy on the Life and Character of Henry Clay, 1852.

5. Address before the Dartmouth Alumni, 1855.

6. Discourse Commemorative of Charles Brickett Haddock, D.D., 1861.

7. Life, Speeches, and Addresses of Rufus Choate; 2 vols., 1862.

8. The Functions and Privileges of a Scholar in the Crisis of the State ; Phi Beta Kappa Address at Bowdoin College, 1863.

9. Discourse Commemorative of Professor John Newton Putnam, 1864.

10. Fourth of July Oration, Claremont, N. H., 1865.

11. Inaugural Address as President of Hamilton College, 1867..

12. Centennial Oration at Dartmouth College, 1869.

13. Discourse Commemorative of the Rev. Samuel Ware Fisher, D.D., LL.D., 1874.

14. Life of Rufus Choate (new edition), 1879.

15. Address Commemorative of Daniel Webster, 1882.

16. Discourse Commemorative of the Hon. George Perkins Marsh, LL.D., 1883.

17. Address at the Opening of the Billings Library of the University of Vermont, 1885.

For the Life of George P. Marsh he had made extensive and thorough preparation, but had hardly begun to write.

Among his numerous unpublished lectures and addresses may be mentioned those on The Spirit of Early English Literature, The Importance of Rhetorical

Study, The Elements of Success in Study, London, The Study of the Fine Arts,
an Historical Lecture on New Hampshire, and particularly twelve lectures on Brit-
ish Orators, first delivered as the Lowell Lectures, Boston, January 4–February
11, 1859.

———

It is impossible to make any complete list of his contributions to periodical literature. Among the most important are :

a. Dr. Chalmers as a Preacher ; *American Biblical Repository,*
October, 1837.

b. The Studies of an Orator ; *ib.,* April, 1841. (See 1, above.)

c. Dante ; *North American Review,* April, 1846.

d. The Spirit of a Scholar ; *Bibliotheca Sacra,* February, 1849.
(See 3, above.)

e. Bartlett's Dictionary of Americanisms ; *North American Review,*
July, 1849.

f. Winckelmann on Ancient Art ; *ib.,* July, 1850.

g. Richard H. Dana's Poems and Prose Writings ; *ib.,* January,
1851.

h. Ruskin's Seven Lamps of Architecture ; *ib.,* April, 1851.

i. De Quincey's Writings; *ib.,* April, 1852.

j. Life and Writings of Dr. Chalmers ; *ib.,* October, 1852.

k. Travellers in France ; *ib.,* April, 1853.

l. The Writings of B. B. Edwards ; *ib.,* July, 1853.

m. The Works of Fisher Ames ; *ib.,* January, 1855.

n. The Ottoman Empire ; *Bibliotheca Sacra,* July, 1857.

o. Walter Scott ; *North American Review,* October, 1858.

p. On Some Indirect Aids in the Cultivation of the Taste (in a series
of articles by College Presidents) ; *New York Ledger,* July 27, 1867.

———

II.

FRANCIS BROWN, D.D., father of SAMUEL GILMAN BROWN, was the
son of Benjamin and Prudence (Kelly) Brown, and was born at Chester, N. H., January 11, 1784 ; graduated at Dartmouth College in 1805,
appointed tutor there in 1806, retaining the position until the summer
of 1809 ; ordained and installed as pastor of the Congregational Church,
North Yarmouth, Me., January 11, 1810 ; elected Professor of Languages in Dartmouth College the same year, but declined ; married
February 4, 1811 ; elected President of Dartmouth College in August,
1815, and inaugurated September 27, 1815 ; he died at Hanover, N. H.,
July 27, 1820. The Presidency of Hamilton College was offered him
under date of March 17, 1817, but declined, May 28th. He received

the degree of Doctor of Divinity from both Hamilton and Williams Colleges in 1819. For contributions to the literature of his profession he had little time or strength. Several of his addresses and sermons were published, viz.: Address on Music, delivered before the Handel Society of Dartmouth College, 1809; The Faithful Steward; Sermon at the Ordination of Allen Greeley, 1810; Sermon on the Occasion of the State Fast, 1812; Sermon before the Maine Missionary Society, 1814; Sermon at the Ordination of Jonathan Greenleaf, at Wells, Me., 1815; Calvin and Calvinism, 1815; Reply to the Rev. Martin Ruter's Letter Relating to Calvin and Calvinism, 1815; Sermon before the Convention of Congregational and Presbyterian Ministers of New Hampshire, Concord, N. H., 1818.

[One who was graduated at Dartmouth in 1819, whose entire college life was thus passed under the Presidency of Dr. Brown, whose keen observation and command of language qualified him to give a sketch of character, whose wide and continuous acquaintance with men prominent in the struggle through which the College passed added to his direct knowledge, whose distinguished talents and high position lend weight to his judgment, and whose personal relations with the son of his College-President were most intimate and most affectionately cherished, has given the following estimate of the father:]

"From the Hon. Rufus Choate,* Member of the Senate of the United States.
" Boston, June 20, 1856.

" My DEAR SIR : It happened that my whole time at college coincided with the period of President Brown's administration. He was inducted into office in the autumn of 1815, my freshman year ; and he died in the summer of 1820. It is not the *want*, therefore, but the *throng*, of recollections of him that creates any difficulty in complying with your request. He was still young at the time of his inauguration—not more than thirty-one ; and he had passed those few years, after having been for three of them a tutor in Dartmouth College, in the care of a parish in North Yarmouth in Maine ; but he had already, in an extraordinary degree, dignity of person and sentiment ; rare beauty —almost youthful beauty of countenance ; a sweet, deep, commanding tone of voice ; a grave, but graceful and attractive, demeanor—all the traits and all the qualities, completely ripe, which make up and express weight of character ; and all the address, and firmness, and knowledge of youth, men, and affairs which constitute what we call

---

* This letter, addressed to the late Rev. William B. Sprague, D.D., was published by him in his sketch of President Francis Brown in the " Annals of the American Pulpit," vol. ii., New York, 1857, and is here reproduced by the kind permission of the publishers, Messrs. Robert Carter & Brothers.

administrative talent. For that form of talent, and for the greatness which belongs to character, he was doubtless remarkable. He must have been distinguished for this among the eminent. From his first appearance before the students on the day of his inauguration—when he delivered a brief and grave address in Latin, prepared, we were told, the evening before—until they followed the bier, mourning, to his untimely grave, he governed them perfectly and always through their love and veneration, the love and veneration of the 'willing soul.' Other arts of government were indeed, just then, scarcely practicable. The College was in a crisis which relaxed discipline, and would have placed a weaker instructor, or an instructor unbeloved, or loved with no more than an ordinary regard, in the power of classes which would have abused it. It was a crisis which demanded a great man for President, and it found such an one in him. In 1816, the Legislature of New Hampshire passed the acts which changed the charter of the institution ; abolished the old Corporation of Trustees ; created a new one ; extinguished the legal identity of the College ; and reconstructed it, or set up another under a different and more ambitious name and a different government. The old trustees, with President Brown at their head, denied the validity of these acts, and resisted their administration. A dominant political party had passed or adopted them ; and thereupon a controversy arose between the College and a majority of the State ;—conducted in part in the courts of law of New Hampshire, and of the Union ; in part by the press ; sometimes by the students of the old institution and the new in personal collision, or the menace of personal collision, within the very gardens of the Academy ;—which was not terminated until the Supreme Court of the United States adjudged the acts unconstitutional and void. This decision was pronounced in 1819 ; * and then, and not till then, had President Brown peace—a brief peace made happy by letters, by religion, by the consciousness of a great duty performed for law, for literature, and for the constitution—happy even in prospect of premature death. This contest tried him and the College with extreme and various severity. To induce students to remain in a school disturbed and menaced ; to engage and inform public sentiment,—the true patron and effective founder—by showing forth that the principles of a sound political morality as well as of law prescribed the action of the old trustees ; to confer with the counsel of the college, two of whom—Mr. Mason and Mr. Webster—have often declared to me their admiration of the intellectual force and practical good sense which he

---

* February 2d. The decision was announced to President Brown by Daniel Webster in an autograph letter, still preserved.

brought to those conferences, this all, while it withdrew him somewhat from the proper studies and proper cares of his office, created a
necessity for the display of the very rarest qualities of temper, discre-
tion, tact, and command ; and he met it with consummate ability and
fortune. One of his addresses to the students in the chapel at the
darkest moment of the struggle, presenting the condition and pros-
pects of the College, and the embarrassments of all kinds which surrounded its instructors, and appealing to the manliness, and affection,
and good principles of the students to help ' by whatsoever things
were honest, lovely, or of good report,' occurs to recollection as of
extraordinary persuasiveness and influence.

" There can be no doubt that he had very eminent intellectual
ability ; true love of the beautiful in all things, and a taste trained to
discover, enjoy, and judge it; and that his acquirements were competent and increasing. It was the ' *keenness* ' of his mind of which Mr.
Mason always spoke to me as remarkable in any man of any profession. He met him only in consultation as a client ; but others, students, all nearer his age, and admitted to his fuller intimacy, must
have been struck rather with the sobriety and soundness of his
thoughts, the solidity and large grasp of his understanding, and the
harmonized culture of all its parts. He wrote a pure and clear English style, and he judged of elegant literature with a catholic and
appreciative, but chastised, taste. The recollections of a student of
the learning of a beloved and venerated President of a college, whom
he sees only as a boy sees a man, and his testimony concerning it,
will have little value ; but I know that he was esteemed an excellent
Greek and Latin scholar, and our recitations of Horace, which the
poverty of the College and the small number of its teachers induced
him to superintend, though we were Sophomores only, were the most
agreeable and instructive exercises of the whole College classical course.

" Of studies more professional he seemed master. Locke, Stewart,
with whose liberality and tolerance, and hopeful and rational philan-
thropy, he sympathized warmly ; Butler, Edwards, and the writers on
natural law and moral philosophy, he expounded with the ease and
freedom of one habitually trained and wholly equal to these larger
meditations.

" His term of office was short and troubled, but the historian of
the College will record of his administration a twofold honour : first,
that it was marked by a noble vindication of its chartered rights ; and
second, that it was marked also by a real advancement of its learning,
by collections of ampler libraries, and by displays of a riper scholarship.

" I am, with great regard, your obedient servant,

" R. CHOATE."

III.

ELIZABETH GILMAN, wife of Francis Brown, and mother of
SAMUEL GILMAN BROWN, was a daughter of the Rev. Tristram and
Elizabeth (Sayer) Gilman. Her father was born in Exeter, N. H.,
November 24, 1735; graduated at Harvard College in 1757, and was
Mr. Brown's predecessor in the pastorate at North Yarmouth, Me.,
which he held from December 8, 1769, to April 1, 1809, the day of
his death.   His daughter Elizabeth was born at North Yarmouth, June
18, 1776; married to Mr. Brown, February 4, 1811, and died at Hanover, N. H., September 5, 1851.

[An outline of her character was given by the Rev. Nathan Lord, D.D., LL.D.,*
as follows :]

   Mrs. Brown belonged to that venerable class of persons who were
distinguished in New England, or were educated in the best habits of
New England, during the last century. Her father was the Rev.
Tristram Gilman, the minister of North Yarmouth, Me., and of great
note in that province. He was a graduate of 1757 at Harvard, a man
of excellent learning, a Calvinist according to the Westminster Assembly; a very earnest and instructive preacher, a beloved and successful pastor. He was eminently devout and wise, and for nearly
half a century was one of the most honorable representatives of a profession which then controlled society, and gave a character to the
most remarkable period of American history.
   Mrs. Brown was one of four daughters, and the third of nine children, of whom but one now remains.† She became the wife of President Brown in 1811, soon after he had taken charge of the church in
North Yarmouth as her father's immediate successor, and five years
before he was elected to the Presidency of Dartmouth College.
   Mrs. Brown inherited largely the peculiar evenness of temperament,
the mildness, gentleness, and amiableness of disposition, connected
with great strength and tenacity of principle and unpretending firmness of purpose, which pertained generally to the times of the fathers,

---

   * Published in the *Vermont Chronicle*, September 16, 1851.—Dr. Lord was
born at Berwick, Me., November 28, 1792; graduated at Bowdoin College in
1809, and at Andover Theological Seminary in 1815 ; ordained May 22, 1816; Pastor
at Amherst, N. H., from 1816 to 1828 ; Trustee of Dartmouth College from 1821,
and President from 1828 to 1863. He received the degree of Doctor of Divinity
from Bowdoin College in 1828, and that of Doctor of Laws from Dartmouth in
1864.   He died at Hanover, N. H., September 9, 1870.
   † Samuel, youngest child of the Rev. Tristram and Elizabeth (Sayer) Gilman·
born at North Yarmouth, Me., November 11, 1790, died in Portland, Me., March
25, 1852.

and were eminently characteristic of her family name. A beautiful illustration of these combined qualities was given in her care of her husband, when consumption, induced by his well-known exhausting labors of office, obliged him to seek a winter's residence at the South. During their whole absence she was his guide and staff and nurse; and between New Hampshire and Georgia, out and home, through the difficult and unaccustomed route, the horse that drew them was driven by her own hand.

Mrs. Brown was a sincere Christian. Hers was emphatically the spirit of heavenly love, the new life of God, which, when associated, as it naturally is in the theology which she accepted, with profound religious fear, subdues everything to itself, but is never subdued, and prevails to the end, because it subordinates all other loves and fears, and the fear of death itself, to God. It gave a distinctive character, not manifested by mere tones of profession, but a consistent religious life, and made her honorable in the Church of Christ. It quickened all her natural endowments; and these, matured as they were by Christian discipline, harmonized by generous sentiments and pious affections, and habitually exercised in genial associations, retained their freshness and vigor in old age. She was a dignified, religious woman, an example worthy of her ancestry, of the name which she bore, the stations which she occupied, and the honor which she received. She fulfilled her probation equally in all her varied conditions of prosperity and adversity, of joy and sorrow, with a simplicity, propriety, and integrity peculiarly her own, and which secured to her —without her asking or thinking to ask—universal confidence, respect, and love. And it was her privilege to die, in a green old age, after a short and not uncommonly painful illness, with the hopes she had entertained from her early youth, and none of the terrors she had sometimes anticipated, in a society which honored her, in a family circle she had long gladdened, and in the arms of her loving children.

She lies in the graveyard at Hanover, by the side of her distinguished husband, and the place of their burial will be gratefully and reverently visited while the name of the institution which they adorned, and whose venerable halls cast their morning shadows upon it, shall be remembered.

———

[The following brief sketch is from the hand of one who knew Mrs. Brown during her widowed life, and loved her tenderly :]

Mrs. Brown was a woman of rare symmetry of character and devoutness of spirit. Her manners were of the "old school"—full of sweet dignity and a tender graciousness, without taint of condescension.

No clouds could linger in that sunny presence. Her broad, sweet charity pervaded every part of her household, which was scarcely ruled, but presided over, with a firmness and wisdom which none could challenge, and none wished to change. Reticent, and self-controlled under the severe discipline of life, every troubled heart turned instinctively to her, sure of wise counsel and unfailing cheer.

Besides those discriminating womanly intuitions which drew one's confidence like a magnet, and offered strong support under indecision and doubt, another secret of Mrs. Brown's singular attractiveness was her love for all that was beautiful, delicate, and noble in art, literature, and society. Distinguished men of her day delighted to do her honor. With all her pressing cares she kept herself informed of the current history of the times, and watched with anxious patriotism the course of our own political affairs.

Sympathetic and generous to an extreme, her hospitality knew no limit but that of the sternest necessity. Sensitive, also, as deep natures ever are, even to timidity, her fortitude always rose to the emergencies that confronted her ; and the sacrifices demanded by friendship, at whatever cost of toil or peril, never found her wanting in the cheerfulness and heroism of an unselfish devotion.

Such is an imperfect outline of the mother, under whose wise and gentle nurture was developed the rare and beautiful character of her honored son.   T. S.

IV.

FRANCIS, second son of Francis and Elizabeth Brown, was born at Hanover, in August, 1817, and died there January 27, 1818.

ARTHUR VAN VECHTEN, second son of SAMUEL GILMAN and Sarah Van Vechten BROWN, was born at Hanover, January 20, 1853, and died there April 4, 1857.

[The following paper, in Dr. BROWN's handwriting, was found in his portfolio. It was probably written in April, 1857 :]

SOME CHARACTERISTICS OF A LITTLE BOY.

I once knew a little boy, very beautiful to look upon. He was of slight frame, lithe and elastic, always in motion, always busy, and capable of finding enjoyment for himself. His hair was soft and golden, and, parted in the middle, hung in waving curls about his head.

His face, when at rest, had a serious earnestness, and sometimes, as when asleep, a sweet solemnity, but for the most part was full of life, merry and gleeful. His laugh was exquisite. Every feature lent its share to the expression. His eyes especially were full of mirth. His eyes were large, blue shading into hazel, and when fully opened very brilliant; his nose straight and delicate, and his mouth small and of perfect form. His other features were regular, full, and soft. When awake, he was seldom still or unoccupied. His senses were very perfect, and he was observant of whatever was taking place ; and when he had once seen a thing done, could tell how it should be done again. If anything were left out of its place, of his own accord he would carry it back, because it " belonged there." If a new dress were worn, or an unusual arrangement of dishes made upon the table, he noticed it at once and spoke of it. Once, when there were visitors, his mother cautioned him not to speak of the new things he might see. He sat quiet and watchful until a little bell was rung of a musical tone, when he started up and spoke across the table in a soft voice to F——— : " F———, isn't that a pretty noise ? " He was very fond of music, and would drink it in (making a little motion with his mouth) with the greatest delight.

He was very sensitive to all pleasurable impressions, and had a capacity for great enjoyment.

His faculties seemed well balanced and harmonious. He was *courageous.* No common things made him afraid. He would lie alone in his little bed at night ; and walk alone to the farther end of the garden without apprehension. He was *self-reliant.* When he knew how a thing was done, he felt able to do it himself, and often, untold, attempted that which he thought should be performed. So he had much practical efficiency, and was persistent to accomplish his purposes. His perceptions were quick, and he readily adapted his means to his ends. He had a quick perception of the droll and ridiculous. Notwithstanding his eagerness and independence, he was very *docile.* There was no obstinacy in him, though there would have been much firmness. He could generally be reasoned with, and was very *trusting* and full of *confidence.* His affections were strong, very strong for a little boy, and his sympathy tender. If his little sister cried, he tried to soothe her, sitting by her side and lending her his playthings.

He had much *fortitude* and *patience.* I saw him when he suffered very much, in his last illness. But though he could not help crying out when he was moved, often saying, " I can't bear it," yet he was uncomplaining. I *never* knew him to complain unless something was the matter with him. When in health, he was very much a master of himself—of his body, seldom taking a misstep or falling—and of his feelings, controlling himself when disappointed. Over all was thrown an inexpressible something which I cannot describe, a manly beauty, a beautiful manliness which exalted him and made you respect him, though he was a little boy only four years and three months old. He died very suddenly at two o'clock, Saturday morning, April 4, 1857. I saw him dressed in his jacket and trousers, lying on his couch, his last resting-place. The soft shadow of death was on his eyelids. His little marble hands were folded on his breast. His countenance was placid, quiet, solemn, and beautiful, beyond the power of language to express. I never saw anything so beautiful. This was his body. *He*, I trust, is with the saints and angels.

All this, and much more which I cannot tell, I saw of my little son, Arthur Van Vechten Brown.

[Separate from the foregoing, but in the same hand, was a description of the illness. A few sentences are here given :]

Increasing delicacy of look. Some failure of vivacity—wishing to be carried up and down stairs ; complains of being tired—complained of his foot hurting him ; kneels in his play, and cannot rise—walks so gently, softly, carefully, by my settee, taking hold of it with his hand, toward the parlor to see what made " that pretty noise " [a flute].

[There follow details of the progress of the disease, day after day. The account of the last night ends thus :]

Suddenly, five minutes before two (Saturday, April 4th), his eyelids droop, breath fails, is shorter, and in a minute or two, without a struggle or gasp, or motion of a finger, stops. The dear, beautiful little boy is in Heaven.

HELEN DUNCAN, second daughter of SAMUEL GILMAN and Sarah Van Vechten BROWN, was born at Hanover, N. H., April 28, 1848, and died there August 17, 1867.

[Of her one writes :]

Her life was spent mostly in the little New England village which was her birthplace, and her character was the natural outgrowth of a good ancestry, aided by the sweet and healthful influences of home, under the dominant Spirit of a Divine Saviour.

The eye beaming with happy expectation, the many charms of face and form, the quick sensitiveness and warm impulses of girlhood just slightly veiled by a faint prevision of future possibilities, sympathy for the suffering, tender care, not for the human alone, but for the small and weak among dumb creatures as well, companionship intimate and unreserved with nature in her varying moods, hero-worship ardent and disinterested,—these are only a few of the evidences of that vitality, purity, and sweetness which seem expressly fitted to bless this world by their presence in it, but are gone out of it before we fully understand or appreciate them. So it was with her whom we now recall to memory. Until within a few months before her death she had the appearance of perfect health, with a vigorous and substantial physique, regular features, an intellectual forehead, and a complexion clear and fresh with the warm glow of youth. As she verged toward womanhood she gave promise of personal beauty of a noble type. Willing to study, and fond of books, she had nevertheless a decided taste for the stimulus of the open air. A fearless rider and excellent pedestrian, full of vitality and of enthusiasm for games and contests of skill, she was the life of a company in out-door sports, and easily without a peer among those of her own sex in all that required a keen eye and a firm hand and steady nerves.

Her modesty and maidenliness were as genuine as her activity, and nothing was more reasonable than to predict for her the noble life-work of a Cornelia or the self-renunciation of a Florence Nightingale.

Child as she was, during the life-struggle of the nation she followed its course with the keenest interest. Her young heart swelled with patriotism, and all the ardor of her nature went into her sympathies for the wounded and admiration for the heroes of the Union.

In social circles she was frank and sprightly, without affectation, her conversation not pretentious, but touched with a vein of humor more pleasing than a sharper wit could be. She was by nature companionable, and in the home circle she exhibited an unselfishness and hearty loyalty to conscience which helped to make life sweet to all about her.

In the days of her youth, before the coming of any evil days, she had remembered her Creator and pledged her fealty to the Father of spirits and Redeemer of mankind. Unreservedly she had committed herself to His guidance and keeping, nor did her faith waver when He summoned her from all her happy activities.

And so the beautiful form melted away, the rosy cheeks became pale and wasted, the blue eyes lost their brightness, the signs of patient suffering showed themselves in face and feature, though the brave heart and cheery spirit never faltered till the day came when she returned unto her Father.

[Another:]

She was active, bright, and independent, from the time she was able to walk alone—very affectionate and sympathetic—greatly interested in the younger children as she grew older, and fond of imparting bits of knowledge. During the war she would put her little sister through quite a patriotic catechism, and the weighty words she thus put into baby lips entertained those who were no longer children. A vein of humor ran through all her letters, which were also earnest and thoughtful. Never idle, her skilful hands were occupied with her needle for useful or ornamental work, and her industry was represented on every side in our home years after the busy fingers were still.

In the spring of 1866 there was a gradual failure of strength, appetite, and color, without any apparent disease. A short journey and absence of a few weeks so far restored her that in the fall she was to all appearance as vigorous and healthful as ever, full of life and active employment. The next spring the same languor reappeared, but gave less alarm, since she had so easily recovered the year before. This time, however, the progress was wholly downward, and with no suffering—no wearisome, wakeful nights—indeed, nothing positive in her symptoms ; she grew gradually weaker, and faded from our sight— falling asleep on the evening of Saturday, August 17, 1867. She knew the opinion of her physicians, and acquiesced without regret.

"It is all right," was her frequent expression. "Are you ready to go, dear Helen ?" "I think so—I trust so." She had been greatly interested in the thought of a new home for the family, and entered eagerly into all plans for the future. She never saw it.

Many young friends and relatives were in the place that summer, and while not losing a particle of interest in all that concerned them, she was tranquilly waiting the call to enter upon a new and higher life. At the funeral, six young girls dressed in white—companions of her own—preceded the casket to the grave, which was lined with flowers by the thoughtful kindness of friends, and overhung with wreaths from the drooping branches of the trees.

V.

WHEN he entered upon his duties as Professor at Dartmouth, in 1840, Mr. BROWN became a member of the family of Professor Sanborn.* In 1841, Mrs. Chamberlain, widow of Professor William Chamberlain,† of Dartmouth, returned to Hanover with her children

---

* See Appendix VIII.

† William Chamberlain, A.M., was the son of General William and Jane (Eastman) Chamberlain, and was born at Peacham, Vt., May 4, 1797 ; graduated from Dartmouth College in 1818 ; made Professor of the Latin and Greek Languages

after some years of absence, and her house was for several years the home of himself and his family.

Professor Chamberlain had died while Mr. BROWN was in College, and his death had been felt as a severe loss by Faculty and students. He was a man of noble purposes and high courage, of excellence and still greater promise as a scholar, and was valued and leaned upon by his associates. " I feel deeply," wrote President Lord to him, under date of July 3, 1830, when it became evident that the disease would prove fatal,—" I feel deeply this afflictive visitation of God. More heavily burdened than others may have known with the unaccustomed responsibilities and labors of my office, I have relied greatly on your better acquaintance with the affairs of College, and on your active services, for counsel and relief, and encouragement in my own duties, and have looked forward with hope to a time when, free from old cares and embarrassments, we might co-operate in advancing our beloved institution. I must mourn when you say that probably you will return no more." A letter of sympathy sent to Mrs. Chamberlain by a committee appointed by the students, and dated July 12, 1830, the day following his death, says :

. . . "We cannot but feel that to ourselves, to this institution, and to the community at large, it is a loss of a very painful kind. . . . He has long sustained to us the endearing relation of an affectionate and faithful instructor. We remember . . . his unwearied labors for our welfare, the tones and looks and words of kindness with which he was wont to hold intercourse with us, his fidelity in the discharge of all the arduous and important duties of his office. . . . We almost feel like children whose tears are falling over the grave of a father." *

With Mrs. Chamberlain and her children, the relations of Professor BROWN and his family were most intimate and affectionate.

---

there in 1820, and so continued until his death, which occurred at Peacham, July 11, 1830.

He was married at Wells, Me., July 1, 1823, to Sarah Little Gilman, daughter of Dr. Joseph and Hannah (Little) Gilman, of Wells, who was born at Wells, August 27, 1800, and died at Hanover, N. H., March 15, 1848. They had two daughters, neither now living, and one son.

* The first signature to this letter is that of Asa D. Smith, then a member of the Senior Class, and the entire letter is plainly in his handwriting. He was born at Amherst, N. H., September 21, 1804 ; graduated at Dartmouth College in 1830, and at Andover Theological Seminary in 1834; ordained November 2, 1834; Pastor in New York City from 1834 to 1863; President of Dartmouth College from 1863 to 1877 ; died at Hanover, N. H., August 16, 1877. He received the degree of Doctor of Divinity from Williams College in 1849, and that of Doctor of Laws from the University of the City of New York in 1864.

7777777777

77

777

[The following words are written of her by one who knew her well:]

It would be a most fitting and delightful task, in this connection, to pay suitable tribute to one of the choicest women of her own or any time, Mrs. Chamberlain. But this simple Memorial is already spreading itself into a family record, and the words must be few. She was a member of the family of Rev. Francis Brown until her marriage, in 1823, to Professor Chamberlain, of Dartmouth College, and her life and interests were closely bound up with theirs. No proper justice can be done to her character in this brief way, and yet one can speak of that rare union of tenderness which could sympathize with strength which could support. One did not shrink from confessing a fault; for, though it might sadden her brow, her true appreciation of the power of temptation or the weakness of resistance brought ever the word of help and comfort, and inspired stronger resolutions for the future. Self-forgetting and self-denying, she spared no effort in behalf of a friend; in sickness, her gentle ministrations soothed and calmed; in trouble or in peril, she was a sure and strong support.

Intellectual and well read, she was ready to meet and discuss the important questions of the day, and proved in more than one instance the wise counsellor, the helpful adviser, the safe guide to younger persons just crossing the threshold of important positions in life. Her own life brought many severe trials, borne bravely in submission to the Master's will, and at His bidding she went to dwell (as her pastor, Rev. Dr. Richards, said) " in yonder magnificence, where all is joy."

[The following sentences in regard to Professor Putnam are taken from the Eulogy delivered by Professor BROWN at Hanover, July 19, 1864 :]

How can the story of what he was be told so as not to disappoint you ? How can the lights and shades of a character of such delicate beauty and such singular completeness, of a life so gentle, with all the elements so graciously mixed, be depicted so as to satisfy your memory of him ?

The alertness of his mind was something beautiful and almost wonderful. Who more quick than he to perceive and sympathize with the most subtle, airy, and fleeting shades of thought ? who more sure to detect the meaning, and *all* the meaning, of the comprehensive and quick-minded Greek ?

His grasp of thought was as certain, as strong, and as positive, as it was quick. It hardly seemed an effort for him to overcome many of the intellectual difficulties which beset the paths of other students. . . . He wrought with unity of strength and purpose. There was no exaggeration, no excess, and no deficiency.

I do not know that such a mind is so apt to dazzle and excite as one that may be somewhat eccentric and intense, but how much more safe it is, and how its excellences grow upon us, and how much more abiding is its influence. . . . He had a quick and sure insight, a power like that conceded to poets, of looking through the surface of things to the heart. Hence, his judgment was sound, and he was not easily deceived or led astray. . . . And do you not remember how quick was his·ear for the rhythmical music of language ; how choice he was of words ; how rapid in apprehension, penetrating to the very heart of a subtle and pregnant expression, while all the delicate aroma of its most secret thought was shed over his mind?

He ever kept the mind of the student curious and active, and refreshed it with a sense of perpetual attainment. In all this he was

---

and in Leicester, Mass., from 1845 to 1847 ; graduated at Andover Theological Seminary in 1849 ; made Professor of the Greek Language and Literature in Dartmouth College in 1849, and so continued till his death. He was ordained to the Congregational Ministry on the same day with Professor BROWN, October 6, 1852, at Woodstock, Vt. He died at sea, between Halifax, Nova Scotia, and Boston, Mass., on his way home from Europe, October 22, 1863.

He was married, August 5, 1851, to Sarah Gilman Chamberlain, second daughter of Professor William and Sarah Little (Gilman) Chamberlain, who was born at Hanover, N. H., November 21, 1829, and died there September 7, 1864.

Professor Putnam's funeral took place October 26, 1863, from the house of Professor BROWN, which continued to be Mrs. Putnam's home for the brief remainder of her life.

guided by an instinct as sure as it was sensitive, which led him to adapt himself, unconsciously almost, to the minds which he was guiding. This occupation was one that he loved, in which he was contented and happy, for he felt himself adequate to it, and he followed with peculiar sympathy and interest those with whom he became thus connected.

He had a ready and brilliant wit. . . . [In it] there was nothing forced or assumed, and nothing reserved for special occasions. . . . These powers he used as charms, as playthings, not as weapons, and I presume that most who knew him but slightly hardly suspected him of possessing [them].

He never thrust himself into a place of responsibility, or sought distinction for distinction's sake. Indeed, he would have much preferred that others, who coveted such things, should have the pleasure of them. . . . Not to seem, but to be, was his purpose. And yet, when the responsibility came, and the duty was fairly imposed, he did not avoid it, but accepted it as a thing of course, and met it with the thoroughness and simplicity which marked his entire life.

In a life so gentle and equable as his, one is apt to forget the depth and thoroughness of conviction and purpose which may underlie that external serenity. . . . His love for that unequalled language and literature which he spent his professional life in penetrating and unfolding never betrayed him to a forgetfulness of the moral defects of the people, or the insufficiency of their noblest philosophy. The love of beauty, and fitness, and grace, though so strong in him, was always subordinate to the love of truth. Though no iconoclast, he would have broken the images, if the only alternative were that he must worship them.

Few lives were more perfect than his whose youth gave so fair a promise, whose riper years so fully redeemed the pledge.

————

[One who knew Mrs. Putnam all her life writes thus of her:]

She was a most engaging child. Bright and intelligent, always lovely and sweet tempered, and as simple and unconscious as she was charming, she was the delight and comfort of her friends. After her sister's death,* when she was twelve years old, she became more

————

* Frances Elizabeth, eldest child of Professor and Mrs. William Chamberlain, born at Hanover, October 4, 1824; died there January 17, 1842.

closely the companion of her mother, but this happy intercourse was ended all too soon, for in March, 1848, the large-hearted, tender mother was called away after a brief illness. Her marriage to Professor Putnam took place in August, 1851. Seldom could two persons be found more fitted for one another. Refined and cultivated— warm-hearted, earnest Christians—they presided over their home and dispensed its hospitalities for twelve happy years. "The heart of her husband safely trusted in her," and she was what he called her— "God's wonderful gift to him." When he was obliged by failing health to travel, the change and rest were almost as important for her as for him. Their pleasant home was broken up, and, each anxious for the other, they went forth hopefully, if not confidently. When he was suddenly prostrated in a foreign land, where neither of them was familiar with the language, her courage rose with the occasion, and she was his nurse and comforter for six anxious weeks. As he was able to listen, she read from their *only book*, the Bible, and cheered the wakeful hours of the night with hymns, with which her memory was stored. "I bless your mother for teaching you hymns in your childhood," he was wont to say. For six months after her return she was able to go in and out among us, and then began to fail steadily, though retaining a generous interest in all about her, and even keeping her characteristic playful humor to the very end. On September 6th she sank into unconsciousness, and through all that night every breath was like the sob of a grieved and tired child.

> " But when the sun in all his state
> Illumed the Eastern skies ;
> She passed through Glory's morning gate,
> And walked in Paradise."

As the morning rays entered her room, the summons came, as if an angel spake, " The Master is come and calleth for thee." And at the word her eyes opened wide, and shone with a depth and brilliancy indescribable, her lips parted with a joyful smile, and she was borne from our sight " through the gates into the city." The lovely, glad look remained till we laid her down by him she loved so well.

The house purchased by Professor Brown, in 1851, remained the home of the family until the removal from Hanover in 1868. When he took possession of it his household included, besides his wife, her son and his own three children, his mother and his only sister, as well as his cousin, his mother's niece. In this house four other children were born to him, and here his mother and two of his children died. The others referred to are all still living.

VI.

AMONG the special tokens of friendship and good-will which gave Dr. BROWN deep pleasure at various times in his professional life, those that marked his departure from Hanover and his resignation of the Presidency of Hamilton College were particularly noteworthy. In the summer of 1867 the graduating class at Dartmouth presented him with a massive chair of black walnut, bearing the words "Dartmouth, '67" carved on its back. The same summer was marked by the gift of a handsome salver and water-pitcher, with cut-glass goblets, a token of remembrance from his warm friends in Hanover. The class of 1881 at Hamilton presented to him a fine set of Mrs. Jameson's works. No such gift touched him more deeply than the last, which is described in the following memorandum, written by himself, and carefully preserved with other relics of the occasion :

UTICA, January 4, 1882.

MEMORANDUM :

This scarlet bag (tied with a white-satin ribbon, and inclosed in a pasteboard box), with the accompanying notes, was brought to me in the early evening of January 2 (Monday, New Year's Day), 1882, by Mrs. John P. Gray, of Utica. We were then at "The Waverly," No. 372 Genesee Street. It was handed to me as a New Year's gift from a few friends.

The bag contained one half-eagle, three eagles, fifty double-eagles, and two ten-dollar and one five-dollar bank bills.

As soon as I know the names of the friends from whom this munificent gift was received I shall record them, so that my children may always remember them. *   S. G. B.

N. B.—To this was subsequently added five eagles not received in season to be placed in the bag.

This gift was accompanied by a graceful note from Mrs. John P. Gray, and by the following letter from the Hon. W. J. Bacon, LL.D., representing the donors :

UTICA, January 2, 1882.

REV. S. G. BROWN, D.D.,

DEAR SIR : In the continued absence of Dr. Gray at Washington, there has been assigned to me the pleasant duty of making the presentation which accompanies this letter. . . .

They [your friends] believe, as I assuredly do, that in the positions you have hitherto held, and not less clearly in the conspicuous one you have just left, you

---

* This list was afterward received.

have done a great and noble work for classical culture, finished scholarship, manly development, and Christian education.

Believing this, they ask your acceptance of the accompanying gift, as expressive of their faith in the things you have already accomplished, and their hope that something more on the same plane, or on lines coincident and parallel, yet remains for you to do.

Wishing you and yours, now and for many years to come, a Happy New Year, I remain, as ever,

Most faithfully and affectionately yours,

WM. J. BACON.

VII.

THE Memorial Window commemorating President Francis Brown occupied much of his son's thought during the latter months of his life. With filial loyalty and careful attention to details he supervised the execution of the cherished plan ; he selected the place of manufacture, approved the design, transmitted the measurements, and arranged for the reception of the window in New York. It arrived in this country and was placed in the Rollins Chapel of Dartmouth College only a few weeks after his death. Toward his relative and friend, his father's namesake, who generously assumed the entire expense, his gratitude was sincere and deep. The following description of the window has been published, with that of the other memorial windows in the Chapel, by President Bartlett :

[From *The Dartmouth*, March 5, 1886 :]

" The window of President Francis Brown is the gift of Hon. Francis Brown Stockbridge, of Kalamazoo, Mich. It was made by F. X. Zettler, at the Royal Bavarian Stained Glass Works in Munich—another of the most celebrated manufactories of Europe. It contains but a single figure, the Apostle John. He stands, his head encircled by the customary *nimbus* of the saints, his right hand raised in the mode of the Latin benediction, viz., the thumb and two fingers open and straight, the third and little fingers bent, the open fingers being said to symbolize the three persons of the Trinity, the closed fingers the two natures of Christ. In his left hand the apostle holds the traditional chalice with the serpent, referring, doubtless, to the alleged ineffectual attempts to destroy his life and the promises of Christ, Mark xvi. 18. His tunic is of the traditional green, with red drapery, his attitude graceful, and the expression of his countenance benign and spiritual, and, as is customary, of almost feminine beauty. The figure may be regarded as a fine rendering nearly of the traditional representation of the apostle. It will bear inspection as a work of art, while the entire effect of the window, as viewed at some distance, is bright and striking."

VIII.

Two members of the Dartmouth Faculty, with both of whom Dr. Brown was long associated, passed away after his death and before the close of the year 1885.

Daniel James Noyes, D.D., was born at Springfield, N. H., September 17, 1812; graduated at Dartmouth College in 1832, and at Andover Theological Seminary in 1836. He was tutor at Dartmouth College from 1836 to 1837; ordained to the Congregational Ministry May 3, 1837; Pastor of the South Church, Concord, N. H., from 1837 to 1849; Professor of Theology at Dartmouth College from 1850 to 1870, and of Intellectual and Moral Philosophy and Political Economy from 1870 to 1883, and Professor Emeritus of the same from 1883 to 1885. He received the degree of Doctor of Divinity from the University of Vermont in 1853. He died at Chester, N. H., December 23, 1885, and was buried at Hanover, N. H.

Edwin David Sanborn, LL.D., was born at Gilmanton, N. H., May 14, 1808; graduated at Dartmouth College in 1832; studied at Andover Theological Seminary from 1834 to 1835; was tutor at Dartmouth College in 1835, Professor of the Latin and Greek Languages from 1835 to 1837, and of the Latin Language and Literature from 1837 to 1859. From 1859 to 1863 he was Professor of Classical Literature and History in the Washington University, St. Louis, Mo.; from 1863 to 1880, Professor of Oratory and Belles-Lettres at Dartmouth College; from 1880 to 1882, Professor of the Anglo-Saxon and English Language and Literature; and from 1882 to 1885, Professor Emeritus of the same. He received the degree of Doctor of Laws from the University of Vermont in 1859, and from Dartmouth College in 1879. He died in New York City, December 29, 1885, and was buried at Hanover, N. H.

IX.

It is a pleasure to make particular mention, in this Memorial, of two of Dr. Brown's predecessors in the Presidency of Hamilton College : Dr. Fisher, whom he immediately succeeded, and with whom his intercourse for four years was frequent and pleasant, and Dr. North, the fifth President, whose retired life at Clinton did not prevent him from being to Dr. Brown a wise and trusted counsellor and friend.

Simeon North, D.D., LL.D., was born at Berlin, Conn., September 7, 1802; graduated at Yale College in 1825, and at Yale

Divinity School in 1828 ; tutor in Yale College from 1827 to 1829 ; Professor of the Greek and Latin Languages in Hamilton College from 1829 to 1839, and President of Hamilton College from 1839 to 1857. He was ordained at Winfield, N. Y., by the Oneida Association, in May, 1842. He received the degree of Doctor of Laws from Western Reserve College in 1842, and that of Doctor of Divinity from Wesleyan University in 1849. He was a Trustee of Hamilton College from 1839 until his death, and of Auburn Theological Seminary from 1840 to 1849. He died on College Hill, Clinton, N. Y., February 9, 1884.

SAMUEL WARE FISHER, D.D., LL.D., was born at Morristown, N. J., April 5, 1814 ; graduated at Yale College in 1835 ; studied at Princeton Theological Seminary from 1836 to 1837, and from 1837 at Union Theological Seminary, New York, where he was graduated in 1839 ; was ordained by the Presbytery of Newark, in April, 1839, at West Bloomfield, N. J. ; was Pastor there from 1839 to 1843, in Albany, N. Y., over the Fourth Presbyterian Church, from 1843 to 1846, in Cincinnati, O., over the Second Presbyterian Church, from 1846 to 1858 ; President of Hamilton College from 1858 to 1867, and Pastor of the Westminster Presbyterian Church, Utica, N. Y., from 1867 to 1871. He received the degree of Doctor of Divinity from Miami University in 1852, and that of Doctor of Laws from the University of the City of New York in 1866. In 1857 he was chosen Moderator of the General Assembly of the Presbyterian Church, (N. S.). He was a Trustee of Hamilton College from 1858 to 1871, and of Auburn Theological Seminary from 1860 to 1871. He died, after a long illness, at College Hill, Ohio, January 18, 1874.

X.

[The following extract from one of Dr. BROWN'S own addresses finds an appropriate place in this Memorial. It commemorates one who was long a colleague of Dr. BROWN at Dartmouth, and who passed out of this life as instantaneously and tranquilly as he ; it expresses his own thought of sudden death some years before the sermon on Albert Barnes was preached, to which Professor Hopkins, in his address, so fittingly alludes ; it notes the unexampled closeness with which one College officer had just followed another, a closeness doubly paralleled in the last two months of 1885 ; * finally, written in stirring times, but for a purpose which forbade the discussion of public issues, its last words are profoundly characteristic of the speaker himself, in their chastened self-restraint, their lofty courage, their steadfast and dauntless loyalty.

* See Appendix VIII.

It consists of the closing paragraphs of the "Discourse Commemorative of Charles Brickett Haddock, D.D.," * delivered before the Faculty and students of Dartmouth College, April 19, 1861 :]

HE had passed the middle point of life, and was on the declining side. Yet who thought of him as being old ? Who would have spoken of him as verging toward threescore and ten ? Who, at first thought, would have classed him with the elders of the congregation ? His sympathies were with the young. He entered into their hopes, and solicitudes, and wishes, as if he were one of them. He had, indeed, a peculiar power of adapting himself to almost every variety of person or condition, but of the young he was never over-exacting, nor disposed to limit their activity or their enjoyment by what was suitable to himself.

His eye was hardly dim; his natural force was hardly abated ; his step was firm ; his countenance was healthful ; his spirits equable— never unduly elated, never greatly depressed. As you saw him once, you saw him always. You did not naturally associate with him the idea of feebleness, or sickness, or death, but rather of a mild, peaceful, protracted life. The more startling the shock of that unexpected announcement that he was gone !

From one of his publications, his Eulogy on President Harrison, I cannot help quoting a few words, because they are so appropriate to our present thoughts :

To death we cannot look forward with unconcern. No one can think of meeting it carelessly and without preparation. Its import is too grave and weighty, its consequences too lasting and momentous. One might wish, indeed, to shun the corporal pang, the pain of dying, the undescribed anguish of the last conflict ; and we sometimes idly covet the fate of those whom death surprises, and by an unfelt blow summons from the midst of life without opportunity to suffer or to fear. But, upon second thought, who would not choose to be forewarned ? Who would consent to be precipitated upon eternal scenes, to take no leave of life, no deliberate farewell to the cheerful sun, and thoughtful moon, and patient earth; to forego the last embrace of those we love, the longing, lingering look of departing affection ? Who would lose the

---

* Dr. Haddock was the son of William and Abigail Eastman (Webster) Haddock, and was born at Franklin, N. H., June 20, 1796 ; graduated at Dartmouth in 1816, Professor of Rhetoric there from 1819 to 1838, and of Intellectual Philosophy and Political Economy from 1838 to 1854. He had studied two years at Andover Theological Seminary with the class of 1819, and was ordained to the Congregational Ministry, November 3, 1824, at Windsor, Vt., but was never a settled pastor. He received the degree of Doctor of Divinity from Bowdoin College in 1843. He died suddenly at his home in West Lebanon, N. H., January 15, 1861.

opportunity of his latest hour for assuring himself of peace with Heaven, and preparation for the limitless and awful future ? It is one of the great common mercies of Providence, that we are brought down to the grave by lingering disease ; wearisome days and nights of pain are appointed to us in mercy.

These are his words, not mine. They linger as if he spoke them, but how fit to lead our thoughts on this occasion ! It would seem that the sudden, unwarned death which was to release him from the world was not that which he coveted, was not that which he thought most suitable to a change so grand and solemn. Yet it seems to me that, though not to be deliberately chosen, this sudden, unexpected, painless translation, from this lower to a higher sphere, was much in accordance with the tranquil tenor of his life. He was not unmindful of advancing years, and, on the very day of his departure, spoke of himself as having advanced to that period of life when one must not expect to be free from sickness, and might at any time be taken away. This was but the natural suggestion of a thoughtful mind, since, to the inquiry whether he did not feel well, he replied, " Never better," and congratulated himself on having enjoyed such excellent health.

There is but one scene more !—a mild, clear, placid winter day ; a gathering assembly, hushed and sorrow-stricken; an extended form, replete with manly beauty, untouched by disease, unmarked by suffering, slumbering as in natural repose. There was no shock, no tremulous jar, no violence, no cry, no anguish, when all the wheels of that life, without premonition, quietly stood still !

.   .   .   .

In a public institution, whose life is perpetuated from age to age, as in every organic body, there is constant change. One goeth and another cometh,—and so the marked features of its character are handed down from one generation to another, or changed slowly and without violence. It never before happened in the history of our College, that the two oldest of its recent officers—one venerable for age almost patriarchal, whom the ear blessed when it heard him, and to whom the eye gave witness when it saw him *—both gratefully remembered

---

* Rev. Dr. Shurtleff, who died, at Hanover, February 4, 1861, at the advanced age of eighty-seven. [Roswell Shurtleff, D.D., was born at Ellington, Conn., August 29, 1773 ; graduated at Dartmouth College in 1799, was tutor there from 1800 to 1804, Professor of Theology from 1804 to 1827, Professor of Moral Philosophy and Political Economy from 1827 to 1838, and Professor Emeritus of the same from 1838 to 1861. He received the degree of Doctor of Divinity from the University of Vermont in 1834. His term of actual service as instructor has been exceeded by only one in the Academical Faculty, that of Professor Sanborn (1835–1859, 1863–1882, forty-three years), and by only one other in any Faculty, that of Professor

86   ·   APPENDIX.

for a public service longer than has fallen to the lot of any of their
colleagues—should have been taken away within three weeks of each
other. Yet, though taken away, they still survive, still beckon us
along the paths of learning and religion, still teach us by their words
and their lives.

We have fallen upon days when there will be required a discipline,
surely not less rigorous, not less exacting, not less comprehensive, not
less complete and generous, than in the past,—when principles are to
be tested, when there may be demanded, not " a fugitive and cloistered
virtue, unexercised and unbreathed," but a virtue which sallies forth
to meet its adversary, and leaps forward to the race, " where that immortal garland is to be run for, not without dust and heat." This discipline, this virtue, may the College ever supply, though one after
another of its revered and saintly masters drop from its honored roll!
May it never fail in any of its high functions! May it always meet
the claims of the State and of the Church, ever moving onward, sup-
ported by its children and friends, and under the protecting smiles of
Heaven!

O. P. Hubbard (1836–1883, forty-seven years), whose name still appears in the
list of the Faculty as Professor Emeritus, whose precise scholarship and ripe judgment are still actively employed for the College in the office of Overseer of the
Thayer School of Civil Engineering, and whose many friends may well hope that
his entire term of connection with the College, already fifty years, will more than
rival that of Dr. Shurtleff.

Professor Haddock was Chargé d'Affaires in Portugal from 1851 to 1855, but
did not resign his Professorship till 1854 ; his term of active service as instructor
in the College thus appears on the catalogue as thirty-five years. This has been
equalled by Dr. Nathan Lord, whose Presidency covered thirty-five years (1828–
1863), after he had already served as Trustee from 1821 ; approached by Professor
Noyes (see Appendix VIII.) ; surpassed by those named earlier in this note, by the
Presidency of John Wheelock, LL.D. (1779–1815), thirty-six years, and also in
the Medical Faculty by Professor Edmund Randolph Peaslee, M.D., LL.D.·
(1842–1878), thirty-six years.

Other noteworthy terms of instruction at Dartmouth have been those of Alpheus
Crosby, A.M. (tutor, 1828–1831, Professor, 1833–1849, Emeritus, 1849–1874), forty-
four years in all, nineteen active ; Dixi Crosby, M.D., LL.D. (Professor in the Medical Faculty, 1838–1870, Emeritus, 1870–1874), thirty-six years in all, thirty-two active ; Edward Elisha Phelps, M.D., LL.D. (Professor in the Medical Faculty,
1842–1875, Emeritus, 1875–1880), thirty-eight years in all, thirty-three active.]

INDEX.

PAGE.

Adams, Rev. F. A., Letter from............. 61
Adams, Rev. F. A., Letter to...................................... 62
Administration at Hamilton, Events of............................. 46
Bacon, Hon. W. J., Memorial by................................... 31
Barnes, Rev. Albert, Sermon on 9
Bartlett, President S. C., Address by............................ .. 17
Bowdoin College, Memorial from Faculty of........................ 41
Brown, Arthur V. V.............................. 70
Brown, Mrs. Elizabeth.. 68
Brown, President Francis... 64
Brown, President Francis, Memorial Window to..................... 81
Brown, Francis (son of foregoing) 70
Brown, Helen D... 72
Brown, Rev. Thomas J., Remarks by 35
Chamberlain, Frances E... 78
Chamberlain, Mrs. Sarah L........................ 75
Chamberlain, Professor William................................... 74
Chapman, Professor Henry L., Remarks by.......................... 24
Chi Alpha, Memorial from 42
Choate, Rufus, Letter from....................................... 65
Club, The, Memorial from 44
Dartmouth Alumni, Memorials from 44
Dartmouth College, Memorial from Faculty of 41
Fisher, President Samuel W....................................... 83
Fisher, Rev. William P., Letter from............................. 50
Friendship, Noteworthy Tokens of................................. 80
Funeral Services 5
Gilman, Samuel 68
Gilman, Rev. Tristram ....'.................. 68
Haddock, Professor Charles B..................................... 84
Hamilton College, Memorial from Faculty of 40
Hanover, Home in................................... 74, 76, 79
Hartley, Rev. Isaac S., Letter from.............................. 48
Hopkins, Professor A. Grosvenor, Address by 9
Leeds, Rev. Samuel P., Remarks by................................ 22
Letters, Extracts from 58
Lord, President Nathan 68
Newspapers, Extracts from 52
Noyes, Professor Daniel J.. 82
North, Professor Edward, Notice by............................... 46
North, President Simeon 82
Oneida Historical Society, Memorial from 43
Packard, Professor Alpheus S..................................... 50
Parker, Professor Henry E., Notice by 28
Presbytery of Utica, Memorial from 43
Publications 63
Putnam, Professor John N... 76
Putnam, Mrs. Sarah G... 78
Sanborn, Professor Edwin D....................................... 82
Shurtleff, Professor Roswell 85
Sketch, Introductory 3
Smith, President Asa D 75